THE THREE OF US

The Three of Us

A Collection of Short Stories

by

MIKE COHEN

BOOKS

Adelaide Books
New York / Lisbon
2018

THE THREE OF US
a collection of short stories
by Mike Cohen

Copyright © 2018 by Mike Cohen

Cover design © 2018 Adelaide Books

Published by Adelaide Books, New York / Lisbon
adelaidebooks.org

Editor-in-Chief
Stevan V. Nikolic

For any information, please address Adelaide Books
at info@adelaidebooks.org
or write to:
Adelaide Books
244 Fifth Ave. Suite D27
New York, NY, 10001

ISBN13: 978-1-949180-14-5
ISBN10: 1-949180-14-X

Printed in the United States of America

In memory of those on whose shoulders we stand,

I dedicate these stories to my family.

Contents

Preface

In choosing the short stories gathered here I couldn't help but be reminded of Aristotle's prescriptive elements for drama: a protagonist, an antagonist, and a complicator. The reader of these stories might also note that Aristotle could have been writing as well about a three person family: mother, father, and one child.

This, of course, was the underpinning of my family's drama where Aristotelian lessons played out, lessons reinforced for me later in literature and on the proper stage in the plays of Ibsen, O'Neil, and Miller featuring conflicted families.

Our drama emerged when my family abruptly left Minnesota to resettle on the West Coast during the middle of my fifth grade school year. Nothing compelled my family to move: no new job, no newly purchased home, none of the myriad events that might trigger a dramatic relocation.

However that sudden departure from the Midwest foreshadowed three decades of deepening discord between my parents. As I grew older I realized that whatever the stated reasons for relocating, a deeper desire on my mother's part had been hidden. She wanted to leave my father. This accounted for her anxiousness to depart even if we as a family were utterly unprepared for what lay ahead.

While I was hardly surprised that my parents separated, the timing – late into their senior years - felt as bizarre and awkward as the abruptness of our hejira west so many decades earlier. My mother informed me thereafter that her life with Dad had been "A Greek tragedy." Aristotle again.

The disintegration of my parent's marriage taught me not to ignore the daily opportunity to experience some personal truth. Though invisible, wounds left by unspoken longings and unsatisfied needs can be lethal.

By exploring moments in which hidden personal yearnings are exposed and blind spots are illuminated (sometimes with discomfort but not without humor) perhaps we may see ourselves with humility and those about us with greater empathy and compassion. If one or more of my tales strikes you as having been successful in illuminating one of those moments I will be gratified.

Motorbike Man

Bernie Rivkin told his son, Arnold, about Mike Crook, the crippled motorbike man, as they walked back to Arnold's car after a Husky-Cougar football game, the last football game of the fall. Bernie loved the fall football games, loved to join the crowd whooping and hollering when the Huskies rushed out of the horseshoe end of University Stadium. Each fall season Bernie's rubbery, lined face would light up when the newest batch of hard, fast kids dashed to the Husky sidelines in their burnished gold and purple-striped Husky helmets. Arnold had never heard Bernie speak of Mike Crook before this day.

Bernie and Arnold had started watching Husky football games together at the University Stadium ten years ago, more or less, after Arnold's mother, Adele, separated from Bernie, late in their lives.

"He's too tight for me," Adele had said. "He is as tight as a tick, and you know it. From now on, I am going to live and spend my money in my way."

The Husky season tickets were in Adele's name because she was a university alum, and she chose to keep the seats. Not wanting his father to unnecessarily lose anything more of great value from the dissolution of the marriage, Arnold had bought two replacements for Adele's two tickets, and thereafter, he and Bernie had sat together at the Husky home games.

When Bernie had serious surgery and had lain recovering, Arnold had bought him a satin, gold Husky booster jacket trimmed in purple. It was a son's small effort to boost his dad's desire to make it through, to make him think about life after his operation. Bernie had mended well and had worn the satin jacket to each Husky game ever since.

As he had sat with Bernie each successive year at Husky games and observed his dad wearing that gold, satin jacket with purple stripes, Arnold had tried to feel that somehow he and his dad possessed an uncommon bond. Yet, Arnold realized—not without a mixture of sadness and envy—that he served Bernie simply as a convenient surrogate for Adele. Bernie never had buddies. Adele had been his only companion.

Bernie was no spring chicken—ninety years old and pretty much deaf. He and Arnold didn't walk to the football games anymore because Bernie's shrinking thigh and calf muscles, their arteries clotted and clogged, did not work very well.

Bernie still drove, and there was a pay parking lot for the disabled nearby the stadium. However, Bernie chose to drive to Arnold's house before each game. Then they would take Arnold's car to the parking lot for the disabled. That way Arnold would be paying for parking when the game was over.

It was Arnold's practice to drop Bernie off at the disabled pickup point before parking the car. From there, Bernie would get a free ride in a golf cart to the Rivkins' seats. After the game, it was still possible for Bernie to hobble the short distance to the car by leaning on Arnold's arm.

In the past, when Arnold had lived near University Stadium and Bernie's legs worked better, they had walked to and from the Huskies' home games. Arnold remembered those fall Saturdays as mostly sunny. He could recall his father and himself strolling together down Stadium Parkway, with its flower beds bedecked with new yellow and auburn chrysanthemums, strolling together down to the old brick stadium bridge, kicking at drifts of crinkled fallen leaves, and smelling the musty puffs of aromas floating in the air from the summer's last blossoms.

Arnold always bought a couple of crimson Delicious apples near the old brick bridge, right before Bernie and he would fold into the mob of Husky fans dressed in purple and gold. The Delicious apples were fresh from the fall harvest, and vendors sold them out of unpainted wooden crates. Arnold would stop for the apples while Bernie continued to walk alone, moving on past the stacks of apple crates. After paying for the apples, Arnold would catch up with his dad. At halftime the Rivkins would sit there in the stadium and chew away on the crisp, red fruit Arnold had bought.

"These are the best I have ever bought. Ever," Bernie always said, juice welling up in the happy wrinkles at the corners of his mouth, clearly forgetting that it was Arnold who had bought them. As hard as he tried, Arnold could never remember a time when Bernie had bought the apples.

There always seemed to be a crowd of politicians in front of University Stadium running for this council or for that judgeship and glad-handing the crowd. Their volunteers gave out free, printed game lineups with the candidates' names plastered on both sides. Bernie would always collect a smattering of free lineups, choosing to keep the one with the biggest print, the one that was easiest to read.

"What a bargain," Bernie would say with a leer. "I might even vote for the guy this year who puts out the best quality job."

At first, years ago, Bernie had taken the Huskies' lineup from the Seattle Times with him to the games, but he had stopped subscribing to any newspaper. Bernie maintained that the Times was too expensive at eight dollars a month.

"I remember when the paper was a nickel a day," he said in defense. "I can get the news on TV."

A few years after Adele had left Bernie, Arnold had asked his dad to pay for his share of the Husky tickets.

"How much are they?" Bernie had asked. Arnold had held out a Xerox copy of the invoice for his father to read.

"They're twenty bucks each," Arnold said, "but the seats are available only if you join the Husky Tyee Club. That adds fifty bucks per game."

Bernie had looked as if he had witnessed a shooting.

"That's over one thousand bucks a season," Bernie had said, shaking his head in disbelief, his hands staying at his side. Bernie's hands were those of a wrestler, which he had been in his youth; his hands were the size of baseball mitts.

"Look at the bill, Dad."

Arnold held out the invoice to Bernie, offering to let him read it. Arnold remembered the old adage that once the consumer gets the bill in his or her hand—big or little—the salesperson can close the sale. Bernie must have heard that one, too, because he did not reach for the invoice. His baseball mitts stayed by his sides.

"I had no idea," Bernie had said. "Your mother always took care of them."

"Took care of" was so far away from "paid for" that Arnold had smiled in spite of himself.

"If I have to pay that much, to hell with it," Bernie had said, his face flushing, his lips pouting Mussolini-style. "I'll just read about the Husky games in the sport section." He still had not reached for the invoice.

"Dad, you don't take the paper anymore."

"Then I'll watch game reruns on TV."

"Reruns are on cable. You wouldn't buy cable."

"Then to hell with the Huskies," Bernie had said, his eyes stupid with anger over the money. Arnold imagined that Bernie's outraged face would look the same if at that moment Bernie were the victim of a stickup.

"We have to join the Tyee Club, Dad."

"I'll pay for my ticket," Bernie had conceded, "and that's it."

But Bernie never got around to giving Arnold a check for the tickets.

On the Saturday Bernie had told Arnold about Mike Crook, the motorbike man, they had watched the Huskies man-handle the Cougars. As they returned to Arnold's car in the disabled lot, Arnold was in a hurry to go. He attempt-ed to speed their pace by supporting Bernie's arm while they walked. His father's arm felt curious and thin, Arnold thought; the veined forearm muscles had vanished. This was the same arm that had seemed so huge to Arnold when he was a boy.

Bernie did walk slowly. What was left of his ninety-year -old legs was cramping on him. His right leg was the worst. Bernie dragged it along as if it were a willful pet on a leash trying its best to head off in a different direction.

Bent at the shoulders, Bernie prodded the ground with his cane at each step, looking for cracks in the asphalt, searching for potholes and loose gravel. They were as dangerous to him as land mines. Arnold had successfully persuaded his dad to carry a cane, although Bernie didn't know which of his huge mitts should grasp the handle in order to support his uncooperative right leg. Arnold suspected that his father fell frequently, but Bernie had not been willing to admit it.

Arnold steered his dad around the clumps of college boys and girls who were hooking up for some later events. The roiling sounds of the slowly moving purple and gold crowd did not bother Bernie a bit because he could not hear them. Bernie's hearing aids, recycled older models, were not a matching set. Bernie plugged them into his huge, liver-spotted ears, from which wild hairs stuck out like twigs. Arnold had urged Bernie to buy a matching set of hearing aids, but Bernie would not consider it.

"None of them are worth a damn," Bernie had said, "so why should I spend any money on them?"

The letter s was a particularly tricky sound for Bernie. When they were alone, Arnold would have to shout so that Bernie could hear his s's.

After drifting for a block or so, Bernie stopped to rest for a while. "The right leg is worst," he explained, talking about "the leg" as if it were a separate creature.

Parked to the side were fancy motorcycles: Harley, Honda, and Yamaha motorbikes—real eye-catchers with satin black, chartreuse, red and orange fenders and bodies, and engine parts covered with chrome. Bernie eyed the bikes.

"I always wanted to try one," Bernie said, "but never had the courage to do it. Way before the war, there was a bike shop in Sioux Falls, next door to Rivkin's."

Rivkin's was Grandpa Rivkin's dry-cleaning store in Sioux Falls, South Dakota. Bernie worked there for over a decade after he graduated from college. Then he started his own cleaners in Minnesota when he and Adele married in 1941.

"The bike shop was owned by old man Crook," Bernie said, staring at the parked bikes. "The motorbike repairs were done by his son, Mike. Mike was a real daredevil. He drove one of their motorbikes all over the place. Mike really knew how they were put together. He just loved them."

Bernie stamped his right leg on the ground, as if a few whacks on the earth would make the limb feel better. His nose was running a little; his draining sinuses gave his voice a warbling sound and added a sentimental quality to his story.

"There were bikes like these—not so fancy, of course—parked all around the Crook's door, leaning on their kickstands. Mike's friends used to hang around there, too, cracking jokes and laughing. Every once in a while, someone would tinker with one of them and then jump on and take off to see how it would go and would tear around the block, swerve back onto the sidewalk, bang down the kickstand, and hop off, leaving the bike there, steaming hot. When there was no one around, I used to go out and swing my leg over a bike, plant my butt on the seat, grab the handles, and pretend I was streaking down River Street at top speed, shooting out of Sioux Falls, past the city limits, flying off on the county roads, past all those old farmers on tractors."

Bernie pulled out a handkerchief from his pocket and tooted his ample nose. With his perpetual nasal drip, Bernie needed a lot of handkerchiefs. This handkerchief was one of thousands collected during his days as a dry cleaner. Bernie would find handkerchiefs in the coat and pants pockets of his customers, and then he would dry-clean and press them for his own use. After he retired, Bernie kept a lifetime supply of free handkerchiefs in a giant box in his garage.

Arnold had tried to get his dad to take antihistamines to dry up the drip, but Bernie maintained that the drug was too expensive.

"If I just knock off drinking cold water, it'll stop. I know it," Bernie would say. The nasal drip went on, as did the warble in Bernie's throat.

A Husky fan jumped on a Honda and cranked on the starter pedal. The motor grunted and popped as it wobbled off past the home-going crowd. Bernie watched the Honda with admiration.

"Mike Crook would just climb onto a bike just like that kid did, kick-start the thing, and take off down River Street, not even looking to see if there was any traffic coming at him. He looked so wild to me—wild, a real daredevil. I envied him, I guess. I guess I just envied his nerve."

It was getting dark, and Arnold wanted to get going. He pulled at Bernie's arm.

"Let's try it again."

Bernie shook his head.

"Too soon. It's still resting." His right leg, his old loyal dog, was resting.

"One day," Bernie mused, almost talking to no one, "I heard that Mike Crook was in an accident; his bike got caught between two cars. Must have tried to squeeze between them. Got crushed but good. He barely survived. His legs were shot. Couldn't swing them over a bike."

Bernie was looking back at University Stadium, not at his son. Arnold had never heard this story before.

"Actually, after the accident," Bernie said, "Mike barely walked at all, only with a set of crutches. I could see him scraping down the street past Rivkin's into Crook's shop, past the motorbikes parked outside. He never got better. I never saw him without crutches. Then your mother and I got married, and we moved to Minnesota."

"Can we go now?" Arnold said. He worried that it was too late, that they were certain now to get caught in the traffic jam on Stadium Parkway.

"OK, OK." Bernie laughed, coughed, and banged his foot with his cane. "Maybe it's ready to work now." A pat for his pet leg, and the Rivkins started walking again with Bernie still talking away.

"A long time later, after the war, I was going down Fourth Street in Sioux Falls near your grandma's house, walking to the grocery store to get something. Your grandparents weren't able to do much for themselves anymore; your grandpa was pretty sick by then.

"When I went into the store, I passed a man in a wheelchair outside the entrance. He wasn't going in; he was just sitting there outside the doors in his wheelchair. He was begging, actually, I think. I didn't want to look at him, but it was hard not to. He looked like Mike Crook. I'm pretty sure it was him. Pretty sure."

Bernie wiped his nose with his handkerchief.

"He didn't recognize me, but he asked me if I could spare a quarter. I said no, and then I looked past him and walked into the store. I think I knew it was him, knew it was Mike Crook, all right. But I still wouldn't give any change to him."

Bernie hobbled to a stop and put a puzzled finger on his lip.

"I don't know why I wouldn't give Mike a little change. I think that was one of the most shameful things I have ever done. Just shameful."

Bernie's head bobbed down as he began to drag his right leg—his misbehaving pet—and look for potholes and loose gravel—look for land mines—while he and Arnold walked toward the parking lot.

Out of nowhere, Arnold felt an urge to tell off his dad.

Why don't you pay for your share of the tickets? Arnold wanted to say. Why haven't you paid at least for the apples or for the parking or even bought a game-day newspaper? All of a sudden, after fifty years, when it's safe to bring it up, you pick on yourself for stiffing a cripple. You bring it up fifty years later when there is no way you will have to shell out any dough to Mike Crook. You just want me to think what a nice guy you are, even though you won't pay for a single thing. Nice move, Dad. Real nice move.

But Arnold said nothing; he remained silently in step with Bernie while holding his dad's withered arm as they walked to the car. Bernie pulled open the passenger door and entered his seat, butt first.

When we get to the tollgate, Arnold thought, *I'll just pull up, block the road, and sit there. Maybe my dad will get the idea for once, and maybe—despite his unreasonable cheapness—maybe he'll pay. Maybe he'll be a mensch about it for once.*

Arnold drove to the parking-lot exit, and the tollgate attendant stepped up to the driver's window. Bernie's eyes were locked on the floor mat, his arms crossing his chest, a safe distance from his wallet pocket.

The ticket taker smiled and said, "All right now. Was it good today or what? Go Huskies!"

Bernie made no sign that he heard the cheer. His eyes were cast down, his huge hands locked tightly into his lap. Arnold saw that his father was cash mute, money blinded, dollar deafened. *The sun could go down, he thought, and we would sit here. And my father would never lift his eyes off the floorboards.*

Arnold took out a ten-dollar bill and asked the toll taker, "How much is it?" Three dollars came back. Bernie just sat there, hearing nothing, his eyes now shut, his hands, as huge as baseball mitts, folded in his lap.

With the car brake on, Arnold looked down at his own hands, the hands that clutched the three dollar bills. His hands were his mother's—no doubt about that—small and dimpled. As different from Bernie's baseball mitts as they could be.

The raging heat that Arnold felt toward his dad dissipated with the setting afternoon sun. For the first time, he could see that there were things out there that Bernie, his father, would not buy and could only envy.

As the afternoon shadows surrounded them with darkness, a snort and then a mechanical snarl from a gaggle of motorbikes started up. Arnold saw Bernie look up with a start and then, with unmistakable longing, gape as the bikes passed their car—grunting, puffing, and popping, each with its own unique voice.

The amplified sound of the bikes, like a squad of bumblebees, seemed to fire up Bernie, whose breath and chest rose to a matching rhythm as the bikers accelerated down Stadium Parkway and around the flower beds filled with yellow and auburn chrysanthemums.

Arnold felt the excitement too. He could tell that Bernie was filled with unalloyed admiration for each helmeted rider, a little of Mike Crook in each biker, each unencumbered by fear and incredibly free. Each the person his dad had always wanted to be.

Bernie broke the spell.

"Can you imagine what one of those rigs must cost?" he said, first frowning and then looking relieved as he touched his wallet, reassured that it was tight and safe and unopened in his hip pocket.

Arnold watched it all as he waited for the gate to open, knowing full well that the old man had been talking to himself. Yet he considered answering his dad's question.

Cost a bunch, Dad. One of those bikes would probably bankrupt you.

But Arnold smiled in silence, grinning for the first time that day as father and son sat in their own places with their different hands, one small pair holding change and the other pair, as large as baseball mitts, utterly empty.

The Cantor's Window

The old cantor and the new rabbi were to meet in the lunchroom behind the office wing of Congregation Beth Tzedek, the House of the Righteous. There was no empty office for the new rabbi, Jacob Kleck, to occupy, so the plan was to split the cantor's office into two new but smaller rooms. It was unfortunate that only one of the new offices could possess the single window of the old room; the other would be windowless.

The cantor intended to keep the window.

For over four decades, Cantor Samuel Krakowski had shared his office with no one; his books were stacked in irresponsible heaps on the floor, and his music sheets spilled over the congregation's piano. The cantor was a gray, fluttery bird and hardly pushy. On too many occasions in the past, he had felt nudged aside by the congregation's rabbis.

At his wife, Sophie's, urging, the cantor had consulted with Rabbi Irving Lishner in the senior rabbi's plush study. They had been colleagues for over twenty-five years.

"Irv, you and I need an understanding," the cantor whispered. "I'm too old for this. I feel squeezed out. At least, I should keep my window."

"I'm going to leave it to you two, Sam," Rabbi Lishner said. "I'm sure our new Rabbi Kleck will be reasonable."

"I can't agree, Irv. Kleck is hardly shy. And his opinion of me? Well. My Sophie had the Klecks to dinner. There at the dinner table, Mrs. Kleck had called her husband Jake. 'Jake, pass me some bread,' is what she said. So I asked, 'Rabbi, may I call you Jacob?' I told him I preferred to be called Sam, that even the children called me Cantor Sam."

The cantor shifted in his chair to momentarily relieve the pain in his back brought on by his confession to Rabbi Lishner.

"Do you know what Kleck said?" Krakowski related. "'Actually, Cantor, I would think it better if we addressed each other by our titles.' Imagine that, Irv. A younger man I have to formally address."

Rabbi Lishner's elbows sat on the desktop, his arms forming a triangle of repose with his fingertips touching under the rabbinical chin.

"You'll work it out. After all, Kleck has taken the Hebrew classes off your shoulders. Remember, Sam, you complained that you were too old to work with the young kids anymore. And remember the Shulkin affair."

The mention of the Shulkin affair made Krakowski wince. In the course of the preparation for his bar mitzvah, the Shulkin kid—whom the cantor found rude, stupid, and unteachable—had called him a name to his face. "Cantor Crackpotsky," the kid had said, and Krakowski had refused to work with him despite Rabbi Lishner's desperate pleading. In this regard, the cantor simply refused to be the politician, and in a rage, the Shulkins had quit the congregation. The Shulkins had been generous donors.

"So what did I do when bar mitzvahs became too much for you?" Rabbi Lishner said. "I hired a new rabbi. That's why we're making room for Rabbi Kleck—to lessen your burdens, Sam. Don't forget."

Rabbi Lishner rose to end the discussion and said, "I know the arrangements are far from perfect, but until the congregation raises money for a new wing, we will have to make do."

The cantor sighed at the carefully pronounced "we," and then he fell silent as he glanced about the chief rabbi's suite. Rabbi Lishner sat behind a medieval refractory table— a deliciously carved, walnut antique that served as his desk. Rich Persian rugs poured across polished wooden floors in a room five times the size of the space that Krakowski would have to share with Rabbi Kleck. Chartreuse bamboo leaves rubbed musically against glass doors leading to a small, outer meditation garden surrounding a small goldfish pond.

As always, talking to Rabbi Lishner made the cantor feel as if he were shrinking. He became aware that his polyester, blue jacket was worn, that the fabric of the coat cuffs were frayed. Indeed, the cantor's wrists seemed to stick out of a confusion of loose threads that resembled dried-out grass on a sunburned lawn. Thinking about his coming meeting with Kleck who insisted on titles and on being called Rabbi made the cantor feel dried out too.

In the Congregation Beth Tzedek lunchroom, the dishes and coffee cups had been pushed away, and the remodeling plans for the cantor's room were spread out on a Formica table flanked by three folding, metal chairs. Pushpins attached a large lithograph depicting the tablets of the Ten Commandments, carved in Hebrew, to the beige wall. To the left of a sink, a Mr. Coffee machine sat on the counter between two microwave ovens. Xeroxed instructions were taped to the wall over each microwave; the one designated for meat bore the picture of a T-bone steak. The other machine, posted with a picture of a milk bottle, was used exclusively to warm dairy products.

Dark and bearded, Rabbi Kleck sat in one of the chairs next to Krakowski. Kleck's arms were crossed, his pudgy legs in an open stance, as his eyes shifted from the shabbier and older cantor to the remodeling plans that lay between them. Both men wore round, black skullcaps. They waited for Alper, the construction contractor, to join them.

Krakowski turned the drawing upside down and then back as he gazed at it. He had once attempted to assemble a model airplane with his son, Adam, but had found the directions incomprehensible.

"It appears there are now two windows," Cantor Krakowski said as, mistaking inside for outside, he pointed at the sketch of the two new internal doors.

Rabbi Kleck shook his head and said, "Can't be." He moved his chair closer to the drawings on the table. "If you look at the plans for the construction of the wall, Cantor, the windowless portion would be closer to the restroom, no?"

Rabbi Kleck understood the plans no better than his older colleague.

"I think not," said Krakowski. "It's the other way around."

"I wonder where Alper has disappeared to," Rabbi Kleck said. "That Alper's kid, Simon, that's a wild one. Last week I had to throw Simon out of Hebrew class, I'm afraid."

Cantor Krakowski had already heard the story. Rabbi Kleck had ejected Alper's middle son, Simon—known to be the hellion of the family and no student—from Hebrew class. His offense was so great that neither Simon nor the rabbi had been willing to tell Mrs. Alper the reason for Simon's ouster when she had come to the synagogue to pick up her by-then wilted son.

Krakowski attempted to get Rabbi Kleck back to the discussion of who would get the windowed office.

"I'm sure Alper will expect us to make up our minds as to who needs the room with the window," the cantor said. "There are two office spaces; there is one window. There are two of us. I have a piano; you have a desk. I need to practice and sing, while you need to write."

Rabbi Kleck adjusted his glasses with both hands, a gesture not lost on the clear-eyed Krakowski. Then Kleck said, "Cantor, my eyes need the light. You seem blessed at your age with better eyes than my younger set." Kleck sniffed for emphasis.

The cantor acknowledged this statement with a bow and replied, "It is the vision of my soloists, not mine, that is of my concern." The cantor had the job of directing the congregation's choir, who performed each year at New Year services.

Strolling around the table to the sink, Krakowski found a cup that he carefully washed.

"Coffee, Rabbi?" he offered. Kleck shook his bearded head from side to side. The cantor continued, "Perhaps the contractor can divide the window equally—in the great tradition of Solomon—between our two rooms."

"Can't be done," Rabbi Kleck stated flatly. "Rabbi Lishner says that division costs as much as building a new window."

So, Krakowski thought, *Kleck has been fishing in Rabbi Lishner's bamboo fishpond.*

"On the other hand," Rabbi Kleck proposed, "a seasonal exchange between us would make some sense. I'll take the room in the summer through the New Year holidays in the fall, and you use it during the winter and spring."

The building lacked air conditioning, and the cantor knew that the bulky rabbi would want to be refreshed by an open window in the heat of a summer's day.

With an absentminded gesture as if he had forgotten something, Cantor Krakowski went over to the cupboard and extracted a cookie tin. He handed it to Rabbi Kleck.

Then the cantor said, "My wife, Sophie's, strudel. Try one; they're fabulous, really."

It did sound as if Kleck was attempting to be reasonable, but something troubled the cantor about the young rabbi's attitude. His insufferableness at dinner, that haughty tone, and his saying "I prefer to be called Rabbi" even while breaking bread in the cantor's home was too much. It made it impossible for the cantor to even consider the offer.

The rabbi nodded his thanks and carefully peered into the container as he selected a cherry, nut, and raisin-flecked morsel. Then he repeated with a note of impatience, "What about the rotation, Cantor?"

Krakowski shrugged. "Of course, at my age, moving a piano is no small thing." He paused, looked down at the plans, and continued, "It appears that the doorway is smaller than the piano, in any event."

Clad in jeans and a blue work shirt open at the neck, Alper entered the lunchroom. His skullcap was firmly fastened to his hair with a bobby pin; this kept it perched on his head. He looked as if he had just completed a massive physical feat; his lips and forehead were dimpled with perspiration; and his big hands, usually at his sides, were jammed into his pockets.

"Rabbi. Cantor Sam." He barely nodded to both. "I know we need to get to work here, but I can't until we can clear the air about something."

Alper sat down on one of the folding chairs across the table from Rabbi Kleck. Usually Alper was a man of energy and few words. Now he struggled to speak as he stared at the table.

"It's about my son, Simon, my Simon. Rabbi, I need to get Simon back into your Hebrew class or else he won't be able to finish training for his bar mitzvah. It is humiliating that I must discuss my son now, but I can't work until this is settled."

"Really, Alper," the rabbi said. "This is not the place or time to have this conversation."

The rabbi looked at Cantor Krakowski, who sat silently just as he had done the day before while Alper had measured his office for the construction of the wall and simultaneously vented about Rabbi Kleck's decision to expel his Simon from Hebrew class.

"Cantor Sam," Alper had confided, "I don't get along all that well with Kleck anyway. Maybe you could just talk him into letting my Simon back in. You could help me a great deal."

Alper had stared at the office's lone window as he had spoken; his look had not been lost on the cantor.

"I really can't, Alper." Krakowski had raised both hands, his wrists cocked in open confession. "I'm sure you would agree that the issue must be resolved between Rabbi Kleck and Simon. That's where the problem arose, and that's where it must end. What did Simon do to get thrown out?"

"I don't have any idea," Alper said. "Rabbi Kleck refused to tell my wife. And Simon says if the rabbi won't talk, he is not about to." Alper had scratched his head. "You know, I spoke to Rabbi Kleck. That man is stubborn; he won't reverse his decision. He told me so."

"We, the three of us—you, me, and Rabbi Kleck—are meeting tomorrow to talk about the room and the window," the cantor had mused. "Perhaps you can approach the subject of Simon's readmission then."

That was why Alper raised the subject of Simon when he entered the lunchroom to meet with Kleck and Krakowski.

"At the very least, Rabbi," Alper asked, "can't you tell me why my son is so bad that he cannot be bar mitzvahed?"

Rabbi Kleck spoke in low, even notes, as if he were pronouncing judgment.

"Here is why. Simon blasphemed the Torah. He committed blasphemy."

"Blasphemy?" Alper said. "What does that mean, 'blasphemy'? I swear all the time. Really, Rabbi, they're just kids. Twelve-year-olds, for Pete's sake. Just a couple of words here and there. Punishment, yes. But termination from bar-mitzvah training? That's too strong. It punishes the whole family."

Rabbi Kleck crossed his arms again, and his suit, too tight for his plump body, strained at the sides.

"I considered that, Alper. I truly did. But under the circumstances, I cannot agree to let Simon return, and that's final."

"Cantor Sam," Alper appealed, "will you tell me? Shouldn't I be told what happened, what my Simon said?"

Krakowski's head swung from Alper to Kleck, as if he were the net umpire at a tennis match.

"Yes, well, Rabbi," the cantor said, "I think it will help us to get back to business if you would explain a bit. After all, we are here to decide on our offices. Why don't you tell Alper what Simon said? Then, hopefully, we can return to the subject of our meeting."

Rabbi Kleck wiped his lips and mustache with two fingers of his right hand.

"All right. All right," the rabbi said. "I was working with Simon and the Epstein boy. Ernie, I think, is the Epstein boy's name. We were in the sanctuary. I had placed the Torah on the altar for the boys to practice reading, and I was opening the scrolls when Mrs. Gertler came in from the front office to tell me I had an unexpected phone call. It was my wife, so I had to leave for a few minutes."

The rabbi stopped and frowned in an effort to accurately recall the facts.

"When I came back into the sanctuary, Simon was still up at the Torah with the Epstein boy, and they were laughing. Simon had his hands—no, his fingers—sticking between the rolls of the Torah, and the two of them were laughing. So they didn't hear me come in."

Rabbi Kleck stood up and cleared his throat. "I heard Simon say something, Alper. I heard him say that sticking his fingers between the rolls of the Torah was like sticking his fingers in a woman's private parts."

"'Private parts'? What parts?" Alper was fairly shouting. "What are you talking about, Rabbi?" Alper was standing up, across the table from Rabbi Kleck.

"Rabbi," Cantor Krakowski said, "I am puzzled too. What did Simon say? What were the words he used, Rabbi?"

Rabbi Kleck shut his eyes.

"Twat. The boy said 'twat.'" The sound of the word coming from Rabbi Kleck's lips was like the sound of a bullfrog croaking under a full moon. "To-at. To-at."

Beads of sweat gathered on the rabbi's forehead as he continued, "I heard Simon say that sticking his fingers in between the rolls of the Torah was like sticking his fingers into a woman's 'to-at.'"

For one minute, no one uttered a sound, and then Alper said, "Well...so." Then he stopped.

The cantor and the rabbi stood there in silence, first looking at each other and then looking at the plans on the table, which lay there open and still.

"I don't know about the two of you," the cantor whispered, "but I need a glass of water."

Krakowski really had nothing to say. After all, the Shulkin affair—"Cantor Crackpotsky"—was nothing compared to this.

Alper was trying to compose a statement that would get his Simon reinstated.

"I have to agree that if had I been there, I...I would have been upset," Alper began. "In fact, I am upset, as much as Rabbi Kleck."

Then he trailed off. His speech was getting him nowhere. He looked lost. Alper shrugged his shoulders and then collapsed in silence back into the folding chair, which took his weight with a metallic groan of sorrow.

As Krakowski stood at the sink, he thought about the Shulkin kid and Alper's son, Simon. Kleck and I are not so different then. Just as inflexible, just as stubborn. Both he and Kleck had hidden so much shyness under their skullcaps. They were no athletes and couldn't snatch a ball from the air. Couldn't even read a building plan.

Krakowski tried to take it all in. He would try to be like Rabbi Lishner on this one: appear to be concerned for both of them while working to get what he wanted. It made Krakowski feel sad to think like this, but he could not help it.

"Rabbi," Krakowski said, "shouldn't the boy be allowed to apologize if he is genuinely sorry? Shouldn't he be allowed to continue his training outside your class?"

Rabbi Kleck was slow to speak, the cantor thought.

"Yes, I may agree to that proposition," the rabbi said. "Some other rabbi could work with him. But there really is no way to train Simon in time, in any event. That Simon is not much of a student, right, Alper?"

Krakowski poured a paper cup full and drank it all. A window was such a little structure in the great scheme of things. The water was cool and clear but with just a little aftertaste of metallic bitterness. He set the empty cup down on the counter.

"I would be willing to try with Simon, Rabbi," Krakowski said. "With, of course, your blessing and that of Alper."

"You?" said Kleck. "You? Even after the Shulkin affair?"

So, Krakowski thought, *Rabbi Lishner has gossiped to Kleck about the Shulkin kid.* The cantor readied a response. But Alper saved him.

"Shulkin schmulkin!" the contractor cried. "Who cares? Simon will write a full apology to Rabbi Kleck this afternoon. I guarantee it. What do you say, Rabbi? Will that be enough?"

Rabbi Kleck looked overheated. His eyes swept the plans on the table looking for a miracle, a vision of two windows, but the drawing continued to reveal only the existing single aperture.

"Well," he sighed, "I really don't have much choice." His beard drifted downward past his collar and sank toward his chest.

"Then should we return to the room design?" the cantor asked.

Rabbi Kleck retreated. "Perhaps, Alper, you can divide the window equally—in the great tradition of Solomon?"

"Sorry, Rabbi," Alper answered. "Not with the budget the board of trustees has given me. That's actually a pretty pricey piece of carpentering. Besides, then the rooms wouldn't be the same size."

The cantor asked softly, "Alper, can the piano be moved in and out of the new doorways?" The cantor's voice shook ever so slightly, as he was afraid that anything he said might block this little notch of opportunity.

"I think it's a bad idea," Alper said. "As you know, Cantor Sam, I just measured your doors yesterday. It's none too wide. And turning a piano in the hall would be impossible."

Sensing that his chance for the window was disappearing, Kleck looked up quickly at Alper, but the contractor wisely kept his eyes on the drawings, turning them about with his right hand as if to give one more consideration to the problem while stroking his chin with his left hand. Then he shook his head with finality.

"I'd have to redesign the whole hallway, actually," Alper said. "Once that piano is in a room, it had better remain there. Does that help?"

Krakowski saw that it was two against one, the Shulkin affair or not. *And Rabbi Kleck must know it, too*, he thought.

"I'll take the office with no window," Rabbi Kleck said to the floor. Then he looked up. "I know you'll enjoy the window, Cantor—Sam."

The cantor heard "Sam" from the rabbi's lips for the first time. Possibilities loomed in his head. He would prove Lishner wrong. He would show them all. Krakowski imagined young Simon Alper practicing his singing of the Torah blessings in the new office, Simon standing under the window, the sounds floating out to the street. Maybe the boy would be a soloist someday. The cantor saw himself and Rabbi Kleck together filling the synagogue with powerful prayers accompanied by soaring music. Perhaps the New Year would bring other changes as well, changes blowing into the room through a single open window. He felt new again, ready.

"Thank you, Rabbi." Krakowski beamed. "This is most considerate of you, most considerate indeed. Maybe a rotation can be worked out if we just put our minds to it."

He reached out and grasped Kleck's pudgy hand in his own.

"What do you say, Rabbi—Jacob, that is—if I may call you Jacob, Rabbi?"

Glue

"I don't know," Jimmy said to his friend Louis. "You can't glue plastic to wood."

"You can too," Louis answered. In the summer of his eleventh birthday, Louis Earl and his pal Jimmy Hertz, who lived next door, built small-scale World War II bombers and fighters from balsa wood and molded-plastic kits. It was August, the long, hot days before school started again. The boys worked in Louis's knotty-pine bedroom, on a worktable that sat below a window ledge where the breeze kept the temperature tolerable.

Louis was constructing a B-17 bomber using a tube of Testor's acetone glue. With concentration, Louis squeezed drops of clear, syrupy adhesive onto wheel axles, wings, ailerons, windshields, and turrets, which he pressed onto a molded fuselage. He was careful never to let glue trickle on the hinges of bomb bays or on the swinging hatches, because they were supposed to open and shut. The goal was to leave no trace of the leaky cement when the job was completed.

The heat in the bedroom trapped the chemical smell of the Testor's swirling around the two of them. The glue smell, a mix of spicy fruit and gasoline, dried up the inside of Louis's nose. When by accident he drizzled some on his hands, his fingers stuck together hard until, with some exertion, he popped them apart. It was like separating a frozen two-stick Popsicle.

Across the table, Jimmy gripped his upper lip in his teeth in deliberation as he held together two parts, the wooden wing and the plastic fuselage, and waited for the Testor's to stiffen. In the heat, Jimmy's nose began to twitch. When he could wait no longer to scratch, he set the model down, and the parts separated with the crackling sound of feet walking on fallen forest twigs.

"See, I told you so," Jimmy said. "Can't glue plastic to wood." His voice was triumphant at the accuracy of his prediction.

"That part takes two, that's all," Louis said. "I'll help you." The two boys pressed their fingers around the joints of wood and plastic that oozed Testor's at the seams like sap from a tree.

Louis had come home from camp with boy talk about sports, cars, speedboats, warplanes, and girls, and he passed it on while the adhesive dried.

"What about this one?" Louis repeated a rhyme that he had heard at night in the camper's tent:

"There was a young lady from Brewer,
Who was riding a bike when it threw her.
A man saw her there
With her legs in the air
And took the occasion to screw her."

Jimmy sniggered across the worktable.
"I bet you don't even know what 'screwing' is," he said.
"Do too," Louis said. "Let me show you something."

The boys put down the model, and Louis went out to the bookcase in the hallway that was a passageway to the living room outside. He returned with a book called The Nude in Art.

Louis laid the book on the table.

"Look at that," he said, opening to a black-and-white picture of a naked woman. The picture was old; it had been taken in the years before World War II. The woman—large in the hips, white, almost alabaster—stood in a classic pose like a Greek statue. Her light hair was in a bun. She had a double chin and a long neck.

"She kind of looks like Mrs. Grover," Jimmy said. Mrs. Grover taught Jimmy and Louis in the fifth grade.

"She doesn't have as many wrinkles," Louis said. He could see the alabaster lady's curved breast, but her nipple was concealed by the way she had turned her bare shoulders.

"I can't see her tits," Jimmy said. Louis strained to see around the corner of the picture to catch a glimpse of a nipple on an alabaster breast.

"I can't see her pussy, either," Jimmy said.

"Her what?" Louis asked.

"Her pussy, dummy. Where you screw. I knew you didn't know what screwing is."

Louis was silent. "Pussy" was a new body part. He didn't know where to look for pussy in the picture.

Sometimes Louis assembled and painted his model airplanes in his parents' new shop, Floyd's Fine Upholstery, located in a rented building near the Earl's small home. Floyd Earl was an upholsterer; he had quit his job with Geiger's Custom Furniture downtown, where he had worked for Everett

Geiger. For ten years, Geiger, who lived a little north of the Earls, had picked up Floyd each morning, and together they drove to work. Now at the urging of Louis's mother, Susie, that was over, and Floyd had started his own business.

The Earls had no employees; Floyd re-covered furniture, and Susie prepared customer estimates and billings. Competition for new upholstering jobs was fierce; Floyd and Susie had used all their savings to pay their bills while the new business picked up.

Louis preferred to work on his models at home because Floyd and Susie stayed late at the shop on many nights and came home after Louis had tucked himself into bed. But each summer evening, Susie would close the window in Louis's bedroom before she went to bed. Each night she would pull together his bedroom drapes, shutting out the distraction of the moonlight.

On Tuesday, Louis placed potatoes in the oven at Susie's direction so that they would be ready for dinner, and there was Swiss steak left over from Sunday. As the shadows from nearby fir and cedar trees enshrouded the Earls' little house, Floyd consumed his meal with control and gravity.

"I talked to Larry at the Shell station," Floyd said. "Larry thinks Everett Geiger wants to open a Geiger Custom Furniture branch out here, near us."

"We're always the last to know," Susie said. She prodded her opened potato with a fork, her Swiss steak untouched.

"Dad, what's 'screwing'?" Louis asked.

Floyd looked up, still chewing the Swiss steak. Susie stopped pushing her fork in the potato. The teapot whistled on the kitchen stove.

"Where did you hear that?" Susie said. Louis saw his mother look at Floyd.

"Somebody said it. At camp, I think," Louis said.

"That word is a vulgar word for mating," Susie said. Louis couldn't remember Susie using the word "mating" before. "I think you and your father should talk a little after we finish eating."

Floyd cleared his throat as if some Swiss steak was still lodged in his windpipe.

"This is your department, Susie," Floyd said.

"Everything is my department." Susie smoothed her dress front as if it had been ruffled by an unwelcome intruder. She rose from the table. "OK, Floyd, you clean up the dishes while I take care of my department."

Susie walked to the bookcase in the hallway to the living room and took down a book titled Human Biology.

"Louis, come in here with me," she said, and Louis followed, perching himself next to his mother as Susie sat down on the living-room couch by a table lamp, one leg folded under her dress. The couch slipcover on which they sat was gray and printed with blue-green tree branches like the fir and cedar branches outside the living-room window.

Fluffy dark-green corduroy pillows, soft and warm, covered the couch. To Louis, the ribs on the corduroy cloth felt like rows of friendly, furry caterpillars flicking past his skin as he moved. He and Susie sat there with pillows behind their backs and one wedged between them. The sun cast late-summer-day gold light through the room.

Susie opened Human Biology, one side on her lap and the other side on Louis's lap. Louis wrapped his arms around one of the pillows and peered over the pillow top at Human Biology. The pillow felt soft, like his mother felt when they first read together, and Louis, smaller then, would curl against Susie's stomach, the two of them breathing in tandem.

"I think it's time that you learn something about females, males, and love," Susie said. Louis nodded in agreement.

"What do you want to know?" she asked.

Louis hugged the pillow. Holding the pillow, he felt he could ask anything.

"Why are men and women different?" Louis asked. "Why don't men have breasts? Why do women cover up theirs?" Then he repeated, "What's screwing?"

The blue-green branches on the couch shone with each question, the dark-green pillows soft and reassuring.

"Louis," Susie said, "males and females are made differently so that when they mate, they can bring different things to their offspring."

She switched on the lamp and started to read from Human Biology.

"Mating is the way living creatures create offspring. Each offspring has its own characteristics, and each mating male and female contribute a different set of characteristics called 'genes' to the new offspring."

Susie drew Louis to her. "Humans mate for life; there is something special between human offspring and parents. Between you, Louis, and your dad and me." Susie hugged Louis. The lamplight in the room had replaced the gold glow of the sinking sun.

"People mate to have babies because they love each other," Susie said. "The bearing of a child is proof of the love a man and woman share. A child is the glue that holds them together. That's love, affection."

Sitting hip to hip, Susie and Louis studied the drawings in Human Biology that diagrammed the way people mated during lovemaking. Louis thought that the drawings of male and female organs as they were linked together looked like photo maps taken from an airplane. Male parts were narrow, curving streams full of silty water flooding into a round, female lake that collected pools of sperm.

There are sperms swimming inside me, inside tiny, inner tubes inside me, Louis thought.

He tried to imagine his parents, Floyd and Susie—and even his granny and grandpa—paired and naked, secretly locked together. Astonishing. Sitting in the crook of his mother's arm, the pillow in his lap, the light shining on the book as the darkening August evening wrapped them together, Louis felt like a kangaroo pup, marsupial in his mother's warmth and heartbeat.

Wednesday night at dinner, Susie and Floyd sat across from each other, their elbows on the table, their chins resting on their knuckles. To Louis, who sat between his parents, they looked like a matching set of dark, brooding bookends.

"Everett Geiger called today," Floyd said. "He said Geiger Custom Furniture is opening up in the North End. He asked if we wanted to sell out to him." He pushed back his chair from the table.

"We can't keep going like this, Susie. We got no volume. Geiger Custom has a lock on the decorators, the professional jobs. We have to stop paying rent on the shop. No cash. I spoke to Burton down at Peoples Bank. They won't advance any more cash against the house."

"I suppose you want to fold up the shop and go back to work for Geiger Custom," Susie said.

"I didn't say that," Floyd said, "but we've got to be realistic."

"I'm sick of you being realistic and me having to live with it," Susie said.

Louis interrupted, "Mom, let's look at the biology book again. I have some more questions about mating."

"What for?" Susie said. "We've read that now." Susie's eyes never stopped staring across the table at Floyd.

"Son, go work on your model," Floyd said. "Mom and Dad want to talk."

Louis felt his face turning red as he entered his bedroom. He should have said nothing; he knew they were upset about the upholstery shop and the lack of new business. It was a bad time for Louis to try to change the subject.

As Louis picked up his B-17, the front wheel mount simply fell off and cracked in pieces there on his worktable. Louis's heart sank; he could not figure out what had caused the model to break. He set the model on the table and walked around it like an examining doctor. The B-17 slumped on the table, its nose-wheel strut askew like a badly fractured limb. There were jagged edges of plastic and wood on the wounded model airplane.

Louis felt ill as he looked at the broken model he had so carefully built. It was a mess. Maybe the wheel broke when I moved it, he thought. He regretted picking it off the table that he had used for model building. Perhaps it had been too soon, and the glue in the joints might not have set.

As Louis reached for his tube of Testor's to reattach the wheel mount and strut in its place, he heard a crashing sound down the hallway, and he jumped up and ran to see what had caused the noise.

One lightbulb burned in the hallway, making the colors of the living-room couch muddy and casting long shadows of Floyd and Susie in the middle of the room. Susie stood over the table lamp, which lay broken on the floor. Louis stayed in the hallway entrance, watching and listening.

"You're not eating enough, honey. That's all," Floyd said to Susie.

"Not eating? Of course, I'm not eating. I realized something." Susie stood thin and dark, her voice rising.

"You're ruining my life, Floyd. You're full of sawdust where you should have guts. That's what's wrong with the business. Not the customers. Not Geiger Custom. It's you."

Louis felt the force of his mother's words; they seemed to make the shadows dance on the living-room walls.

"You care only about yourself." Susie's lips were pulled back, teeth exposed. "You want to fail so that you can go back to work for Geiger so that you can be a little yes-man with your little lunch bag waiting for your boss to do you a big favor and drive you to work."

Her voice was close to a warning siren. Louis saw his mother lean on the couch where together she and Louis had talked about love and mating.

"What do you want me to do, Susie?" Floyd's voice was genuine and confused.

"Well," she said, "call up Mr. Geiger, the big shot, and beg for your job back. Go back to him. Just get away from me." Susie shook in gusts. Louis's head began to spin with the dancing shadows. Floyd stepped over the broken lamp toward Susie.

"Susie, you don't mean this." Floyd stretched his arms out, as if to console her. Susie pushed away his hands with finality.

"Get away from me, Floyd; I won't let you soft-soap me this time." She turned to retreat from the room.

Louis dashed to Susie, past the dancing shadows on the walls, and grabbed on to Susie's waist.

"Don't fight anymore," he said, holding on to his mother the way a sailor would hold onto a mast in a typhoon.

Susie thrust Louis aside hard.

"Why are you here?" she said. "Get out now. Oh Christ! What am I doing? Leave me alone, both of you."

Susie snatched up a dark-green pillow, the same ribbed-corduroy-covered pillow that she and Louis had sat on, hugged on, mother and child, as they talked about love and mating. She drew back her arm and wildly flung the pillow, soft and pliable, and it wobbled through the air, directionless, until it glanced off Louis's face with a plop and then fell to the floor.

Louis felt the pillow strike his face with force, the caterpillar ribs of corduroy imprint on his cheeks. It was as if with the velocity of Susie's throw, the pillow's corduroy cover had hardened. It was as if his mother had struck him in the face with the flat of her open hand.

As Susie had collapsed on the couch, howling like a creature caught in the clamped teeth of a steel trap, Louis fled the room. The howl followed him into his bedroom, but he found that the sound was echoing from his mouth as well.

On the worktable washed by moonlight, Louis saw the broken pieces of his B-17 model. Real planes are sheets of pure aluminum and held together by rivets and bolts, he thought. Glue can't hold plastic to wood any better than plain paste. He knew now that it took more to bind together things that were different. But he did not know how to join that which had separated on its own.

The broken B-17 was now a thing to be discarded; there was no comfort in the assembling of the thing anymore. With hands that seemed older, Louis tossed the useless tube of Testor's into the wastebasket, lay on his bed in the moonlight, and waited for his mother's nightly visit. But this night she did not come to his room, and when Louis found sleep, the drapes in his room were untouched, still pulled back. The window remained unclosed, too, and the damaged room lay bare to the uncertain night air and to the passing shadows outside.

Fallout

In the rearview mirror of the Battlellac, the car we are riding in, I can see myself wearing my 3-D glasses. There is a red plastic lens over my right eye and a blue plastic lens on the left. I need my 3-D glasses to read *Atomic Tales: The Revenge of Superchief,* my 3-D comic book that lies open on the car seat next to me.

"The Battlellac" is what I call the Cadillac. It is a kind of battleship with wheels, US Navy–gray outside with chrome rocket cannons sticking out of the grille. Nobody gets in front of the Battlellac. They could get rammed. And the cannons may be atomic.

My mom smokes Pall Mall cigarettes as she drives the Battlellac across Montana. The upholstery smells like cigarettes. "No smoking when I'm in the car," Dad used to say. Dad is not with us on this trip, and Mom smokes all the time.

The notched sides of my 3-D glasses where they hang on my ears are shaped like the fender fins on the Battlellac. My eyes in the mirror look like they are covered by red and blue food wrappers. I am sure there is lead in my 3-D glasses. Lead stops radiation.

The sky rumbles red and blue through my 3-D glasses.

"Thunderstorm," Mom says, her right hand holding the steering wheel, her left elbow sticking out the open window. She moves her arm inside and pushes the electronic button, and the window shuts before the rain starts. A boom fills the car.

"Do they drop A-bombs on Montana?" I ask.

My comic book, *Atomic Tales*, has a big mushroom cloud on the front cover. Inside the comic, an air-force plane drops an A-bomb on an Indian reservation. It's a mistake, they say, but I don't think so. The air force calls the A-bomb explosion a "Broken Arrow," so I think that bombing the tribe might have been on purpose to break the arrows of the tribe.

Anyway, radioactive fallout is all over the reservation, and the tribe's dead bodies are in 3-D everywhere. The chief is the only survivor. He goes on the warpath to find the air-force general who ordered the A-bomb dropped. The radiation gives him superpowers, and he becomes Super-chief.

In 3-D, Superchief leaps out of the picture frame onto the page, thrashes soldiers, and flies over buildings. Alive. I am pretty sure that Atomic Tales is a true story.

"Does our car have a Geiger counter?" I ask. "*Atomic Tales* says that Geiger counters show fallout."

"Sorry, no Geiger counters," my mother says.

"I don't really know what fallout looks like," I say. "I think we should get a Geiger counter to check for fallout in the car."

"I should never have allowed that comic book," my mom says. "You take those glasses off your face right now."

Mom wears a pleated skirt and a sleeveless blouse with little brown dots on it. If I stare at the dots, my eyes swim, and I get dizzy. Mom blows smoke as she talks.

"They'll damage your eyes," she insists.

My mom is wrong about 3-D glasses. If an A-bomb went off, you could watch through the 3-D glasses, and your eyeballs wouldn't melt. I sneak on my 3-D glasses every chance I get as we drive across Montana.

Mom is driving to Custer's Last Stand, and I help her by looking for the arrow-shaped signs that point the way. Custer's Last Stand is way off the road, west, way outside radio stations, way off the beaten path.

"Why are we going to Custer's Last Stand?" I ask. "Are we staying there long?"

"I told you," Mom says. "We might move out here, move out west. And Custer's Last Stand is history. A massacre happened there. It is the real wild West."

"Maybe we won't then?" I wave my fingers in front of my face and make them red and blue.

"Go to Custer's?" Mom puffs away.

"No. Maybe we'll go home." I lie down on my car pillow in the closed-window heat and listen for an A-bomb.

"Maybe, yes; maybe, no. Maybe we'll see some Indians."

Mom barely talks louder than the rain outside the car. Mom starts us traveling late. In the old days when we went on vacations together, Dad used to drive early in the morning. I like sleeping late.

My tongue finds a shred of ham that has been stuck in my teeth since breakfast in Miles City. The ham tastes sweet and salty, and I dream about my next breakfast. I dream about food all the time. What if you were locked in a warehouse with your favorite food? Would it be hamburgers, maybe, with lettuce, pickles, tomatoes, and mustard? Or breakfast? I would always choose ham and eggs. With hashbrown potatoes.

In Miles City I wore my 3-D glasses at breakfast. Mom ate no food; she just smoked a cigarette with her coffee. My cinnamon roll had sugar icing on the top whipped into little peaks. It had uranium fallout in it; you could tell when you looked through the 3-D glasses. The glow of the icing made my teeth ache. I read in *Atomic Tales* that fallout is everywhere.

The sky rumbles again. "Was that an A-bomb?" I ask.

The hills drip rain; the road is soft, black, and greasy. It always rains after an A-bomb attack. I wonder if the radioactive rain soaks into the tires or if fallout gets in when the rain splats on the car windows. I am on the lookout for signs like broken arrows, signs of A-bomb targets.

"We are still in Mountain Standard Time." Mom puffs away. "A good time to make tracks. Kit Carson probably made tracks in Mountain Standard Time too."

Mom is trying to be cheerful in the heat and rain. I push the 3-D glasses back on my nose so that my eyelashes touch the lens.

"Louis has eyelashes like a girl," Mom once told a babysitter when I was little. If I blink, my lashes brush the red and blue lenses like a windshield wiper. I flip the corner of my glasses so that the lenses move up and away from my eyes; then I let the glasses fall back onto the bridge of my nose. On. Off. Like a wall switch.

Mom just drives while I study the two-lane asphalt road in red and blue. Trucks creeping along slow us way down. I can see around the trucks with my 3-D glasses.

"Pass now," I urge.

Mom waves her right hand in the air, cigarette in her lips, and says, "OK, OK." She tromps on the gas and the Battlellac lumbers around the truck.

"You should try on my 3-D glasses," I offer.

"I don't want to see things in 3-D," she says. "Getting around in real life is hard enough."

I am hungry, but Mom doesn't want to eat much. She just smokes.

I wonder where Dad is this minute. Dad thinks that an underground fallout shelter in our backyard is a good idea. Before Mom and I left for Custer's Last Stand, Dad was out in back pounding wooden stakes into our backyard lawn.

"This is where the bomb shelter will go," he said. Dad wears a hat with a brim whenever he works outside in the sun. Dad tied a long piece of white string around one of the stakes. Mom watched Dad from the porch as she smoked a cigarette.

"This is the stupidest thing you have ever done," Mom said. "The neighbors will think we're crazy."

"That may be." Dad walked around, stretched the string to each stake, and then wrapped it tightly, making a house with string sides. "Fine. Let them laugh away. We'll see who's laughing when the time comes. And I'm putting a no-smoking sign on the door. There won't be any cigarettes allowed inside here, period."

I didn't think that an A-bomb shelter was a bad idea, although I never heard an A-bomb go off in my home—only maybe now in Montana.

With my glasses right up against the side window, I can see a rain cloud speeding alongside the Battlellac. The cloud is shaped like a face, like Superchief's face, flying in 3-D. White haze—it must be radioactive—streaks over the chief's face. The Battlellac's windshield wipers thump words into my chest: "Go back; go back; go back." Or maybe it's the cloud-face warning me. The thumps get louder, and I get frightened the way I did at the movies when Frankenstein walks out of the castle. So I blink my eyelashes quickly, first against the blue and then against the red. That sweeps the cloud-face away and empties the gray sky.

"I need to go to the bathroom," I say through my 3-D glasses.

"We are almost there," Mom says. "Custer's Last Stand."

"Almost there," she repeats in her smoky voice. "Just up the road."

There is a sign shaped like an arrow—not broken—that says "Custer's Last Stand," and Mom turns the Battlellac off the main highway. There are no other town names on the sign. Custer's Last Stand must be the end of the road; maybe that is why the cavalry all died there, massacred. There must have been nowhere else to go.

Cavalry. I used to say "calvary" until Julian Packwood, who lives across the street from my granny, made me feel stupid when we were playing cowboys and Indians.

"Calvary is where your people crucified our Lord," Julian said and then pushed me in the chest with his pointer finger. "So don't say 'calvary' when you mean 'cavalry.'" I like Julian a lot, but sometimes, I think "calvary" just for spite.

The rain has stopped pouring, and the wet road shrinks in front of the Battlellac. A creek gully curves next to the road. The car has to slow down. Mom puts down her window.

"Because of the heat," she says, as we creep along slow and hot, cars in front, cars behind.

No air can slip inside at this speed. My skin is thistle sticky, my pants legs damp. They won't slide over the felt seat. I can't sit still; my legs twitch from the heat. I want to wave my hands and arms and whoop out loud.

"Stop that," Mom orders. "You are trying to irritate me. I'm doing this for you. This is special, Louis. You'll feel this was worthwhile. You'll see."

The road ends at the bottom of a hill in a gravel parking lot surrounded by yellow fields. At the far end of the parking lot is a large building. The cars leaving and arriving pass each other, but nobody waves. All the cars need a wash and wax.

My mom steps out of the Battlellac. I fold my 3-D glasses and place them in my back pocket.

"There's the center," Mom says, taking my hand. As she and I walk toward the building, I grab the front of my pants with my other hand, and Mom sees me.

"So, go to the toilet if you have to."

When I was real little, that meant I could go to the bathroom with her, but not anymore. "You stare too much," she says to me when I asked to go into the women's with her. It's true. With Mom, I could see women's bare legs with crumpled underpants under the stall doors.

The men's bathroom at Custer's Last Stand is past the souvenir shop, past the postcards. On the walls of the hallway, there are black-and-white pictures everywhere, pictures of dead cavalrymen lying on the ground. Old pictures. Even when I look at them through my 3-D glasses, the dead stay inside the picture frames. They don't come alive, like Superchief flying off the page in Atomic Tales.

The bathroom has a long, white trough and a lot of flies. The floor around it is all wet. Because of the fallout, I worry about my shoelaces getting soggy. I try not to lean against the trough edge while I pee.

Outside, I don't see Mom, but there is a girl walking around. She looks about ten or eleven years old and is wearing a striped T-shirt, and her front teeth overlap a little.

"Hey, kid." She squints, her hands tucked in her jeans, hip sticking to one side. "Seen the guns yet?"

"What guns?" I only remember the pictures of the dead soldiers.

"I saw them in there." She points. "Past the souvenir shop over there."

"Have you ever seen an atomic bomb?" I ask. "I think one went off this morning. I heard the boom. I saw the rain and the fallout."

She squints again. "What are you talking about, kid?"

"Do you have 3-D comic-book glasses?" I ask. "The glasses help you see the fallout, but you have to look through glasses to see it. I brought some." I hold out my glasses, the red and blue plastic blinking on and off like a neon sign in my hand. "Want to try them on? They change everything."

"Comics are dumb," the girl says, but she puts the 3-D glasses on her nose anyway. Reflections down her cheeks make her look like she is blushing red and blue while she waves her hands back and forth in front of her face.

"I don't see no atomic anything." She looks disappointed. "Where are you from anyway?"

I don't think it is a question by the way she says it, but I try to answer. I want to know the answer myself.

"I used to be from Minnesota," I say, "but now I might be from a new place."

She hands the glasses back to me. "I think you're from Creepsville," she says and runs off toward the cars in the gravel lot. I watch her jeans; she runs like a boy.

"Got to go. See ya," I say to the girl, although she is already gone. I never asked her name; at least I can't remember that I did. I never asked her where she was from, either. It doesn't mean as much now, since I am unsure where I am from.

Mom is waving at me with one hand, hard like a windmill. She holds out the other for me to take.

"We'll walk together," she says. "The monument is this way; the real last stand. This is true life, real history."

The gravel crunches under my foot. The gravel has puddles of brown mud, and wooden arrows point through the high grass toward the monument. One of the arrows is cracked in half. Quickly I slip on my 3-D glasses.

"There's a broken arrow," I warn.

"There are vandals everywhere," my mom says. "Even at national parks. It's terrible."

At the Last Stand monument, my mother lights a cigarette, and I watch the meadow change from yellow to red and blue through my glasses. The wind swishes the grass and slams it around in waves. The grass turns dark when it sways, stays light where it stands still. I am sure that the dark part must be the fallout.

I see the waves crash into a body, a sprawled body that separates the grass, arrows sticking out of the body. The arrow feathers wave in the 3-D wind.

As the wind parts the grass, I see broken arrows lying on the ground. I see other 3-D dead cavalry in the dark, swaying grass, uniformed bodies stacked up, arrow pincushions. The summer bugs whiz around the bodies.

"So this monument marks the spot where it happened." My mother blows smoke. Without 3-D glasses, she can't see the bodies in the grass, can't see the fallout.

I look up the path through my glasses. There is an Indian with a blue and red face like Superchief's, but he is wearing jeans and a T-shirt and a cowboy hat, no feathers. His boots are covered with that mud from the path—red through the right eye, blue through the left eye. Radioactive. He looks at me, or maybe he looks at my scalp. He laughs, his eyes cold. I think he is enjoying all the dead soldiers. I can't see his hands, but he might hold a tomahawk, a tomahawk with a blood-blackened blade.

I step back and tug on my mother's sleeve.

"I want to go home." The sound doesn't come out of me right. It slips a little, so I tug at my mother's arm to be clear. "Let's go back now. Can't we?"

"What are you talking about?" Mother's smoke is sucked away by the wind.

"I miss Dad. I miss Granny. I miss Julian. Can't we go back?" I am wiping my nose now on the back of my hand and pushing my 3-D glasses up at the same time.

"No, we can't go back there, for reasons that you'll have to leave to me. That's all. We're going to a new place that you'll like just as well. You'll see." She lights a new cigarette and snaps her purse shut.

When Mom and Dad were together, I could figure out which one would agree with me and side against the other. But here with Mom, I am all alone.

"I want you to buy some postcards," Mom says. "Send one to Granny. She'll enjoy knowing that this trip was good for you educationally. Custer's Last Stand is in all the books, you know. Send one to your father if you like."

"I don't want to send postcards home. I want to go home."

"Don't you care about your granny?" Mom shakes me by my arms. "She will never be here, and if you thought for one minute, you would know how much it would mean to get a card from her only grandchild. If you don't care about her, then don't get a card. I couldn't care less."

Mom starts walking fast toward the parking lot, pulling me along.

"If we had just stayed on the road, we could have been in Missoula by now," she says. "But we didn't so that Mr. Grateful here could see Custer's Last Stand. But I guess you can't please some people, ever."

I try to keep up with Mom. I want to ask if she, my mother, wants to be together with Dad and with me again, all of us together again, but the words in my throat won't come out. The only thing I can do while I walk alongside her and hold her hand is to stare through my 3-D glasses. I look at the red and blue hills with Custer's monument behind. I see my mother next to me in red and blue, the colors of my grandmother's apron, the colors of the clown wallpaper in my bedroom at home. All the time the wind blows the grass and the fallout around the bodies and the broken arrows.

After Custer's Last Stand, Mom and I stay in a Missoula motel. I dream we are back home in the new fall-out shelter Dad built: Mom, Dad, and me. We are so happy to be inside. Over my bed in the shelter, there is a picture of cavalrymen being chased by Indians, but they are never massacred; they are never dead.

In the corner of the shelter, a periscope shows the surface where atomic winds have piled radioactive fallout on streets, cars, lawns, and houses. But down here, underground, the air is still, and the warm buzz of a Geiger counter makes me sleepy. It says, "Don't leave," and I pull my red and blue quilt around me and fall asleep, my 3-D glasses sitting on the table, waiting and ready.

I Wrote a Poem for My Best Friend's Wedding

First of all, I have to thank Mrs. Popkin. I mean, Alice. I know. I'll try not to do that again, Alice. But it's hard to call someone Alice who drove you to Hebrew class, not to mention dancing lessons, when you were a little girl. Anyway Mrs. Popkin—Alice—called to me in Berkeley and said, "Jackie Blumenfeld, you know how disappointed Celeste and Ben would be if you sat on your hands and didn't say something at the rehearsal dinner before their wedding." Something perky and funny. Little stories.

"After all," Mrs. Popkin—Alice—said to me, "Jackie, you're Celeste's best friend."

The trouble is talking is Celeste's game. Celeste is going to be a great lawyer. That's it; let's hear some applause for that one. That's good. I'm pretending that the clapping is for me and for the poem that I wrote but that you haven't heard yet.

Talking like this is hard for me, especially with this microphone that Alice handed me. Talking like this is not something that I do well. I'm too dreamy. But I love Celeste so much that I couldn't say no.

Right now my knees are shaking, but I'm here, Celeste. I promise I'll do my best. Really. Because if I hadn't been Celeste's sister for all these years and watched her fearlessness and commitment to getting what she wanted no matter what, my dreams would have been so small, so cramped.

Oops. Sorry for hitting the microphone. I lost my balance. You know, it is really hard to hold the microphone in one hand and the champagne in the other. Now that I've spilled my last one, it's time for a refill to get me going again.

Waiter! Thanks. That's good. And I truly believe that this cheap stuff does swallow easier than Dom Pérignon. Oops, Mrs. Popkin—I mean, Alice. Sorry about that.

Remember, I wouldn't be here without your call.

And all of your family, Celeste, they are all here: Uncle Mort, Auntie Faye, Grandma Popkin, all those Popkin cousins Celeste always talked about. And Ben's family too. I can see that you are all waiting for me to tell about my friends, Celeste and Ben, who are marrying tomorrow.

Where does this start? It starts when my mom and dad divorced, and Mom and I went to LA. Celeste and I were the only Jewish kids in our third grade. Then we went to camp together. By high school I loved Celeste as if she were part of my own skin, my own soul. So Celeste and I have been sisters forever, since grade school, as you can see.

I have always been so proud of Celeste. In high school she was the editor of the newspaper and on the cheer squad, and of course, she got into Princeton.

I was French club secretary. That's it. "FCS." Right by my name in the high-school annual.

Anyway, in high school Celeste always called me when she got home from her dates and told me all the details about the party and the people there, all about her latest boyfriend, the smell of his cologne, the car they drove in. She always promised that I could go next time, but we never seemed to.

No biggie.

In college we always saw each other when Celeste came home from the East. I was so thrilled to have my Celeste back when we went to grad school at Berkeley, and together we rented that cute little pad on Cheswick Street. That's where we both met Ben.

I met him first.

No biggie.

Anyway, after Mrs. Popkin—Alice (there I go again)—called me and asked me to talk tonight, I went to Muriel, Muriel Gardino. She's my friend. And my therapist. I decided against a Jewish counselor. Too much approval involved. I chose Muriel, because I sensed we could have an adult relationship right off the bat. She was so up-front. I know, it's a sixties term. I mean, it doesn't have to be just shouting "shit and fuck" in a crowded room, you know.

What's that? You can't hear me in the back of the room, Grandma Popkin? I'll speak up, I promise. *Is this better?*

Anyway, Muriel says that being up-front means being honest. So I said to Muriel—after Alice called—"How can I stand up at Celeste's wedding and say what I feel inside?" And that Muriel, she broke form. Counselors are never to tell you what to do, but Muriel is really my friend.

She said, "Just be up-front."

So, Muriel, here's to you.

I'll try. Here goes.

Celeste and I used to lie in bed late at night, just like those Jane Austen characters. We would duck under the covers and share our dreams, giggling all the time about what our boyfriends might be like. You know, their bodies. We swore an oath that we would never tell our secrets. Our "erotic naïveté," I think Celeste called it. Maybe it was just my naïveté.

Well, Celeste, I think I am going to break my oath.

Celeste, how could I not tell them that you were amused at how easily your boyfriend's pants got stiff when you would get up from the couch and lock the door? Do you remember you used to tell me that you dreamed of being a stripper and that you longed to learn how to open pants zippers with your teeth?

Alice, don't you dare try to take the microphone from me! Just keep pouring the champagne, remember. Then sit your fat behind down, OK?

OK.

Anyway, those were the kind of sweet fantasies Celeste and I shared for years. Knowing you, Celeste, has changed me.

"Be up-front," Muriel said. That's my goal.

It did upset me. I'll be honest. It did upset me, Celeste, when you moved out of our unit and in with Ben, left me right in the same building. Ben and I had talked, too, you know, before then—deep talks on long walks together. Just the two of us. Remember, Ben? You told me that you might teach math; no money in teaching, is there? But—up-front—Ben, you would be a good math teacher too.

What business are you in, Mr. Popkin, wholesale toys? That is what the Popkins do, isn't it? Toys? And Ben's going to be in the business too!

Lechayim! Now some more champagne! I will read my poem for you, Celeste, if somebody will refill my glass.

What? The champagne is gone? Let's move to bourbon. Bartender, brown one up for me so I can get to the poem.

I must ask you, Celeste, how did you ignore Ben's smelly socks, the soiled underpants piled in the corner of the room, the golf clubs, the beer bottles, all those sexist posters of female tushies in bikinis on the wall?

Then I questioned myself: why had I ignored Ben's insipid laugh, his talking all the time about sports? Could I have mastered that look of wonder—Celeste, I really admire you for that one—you looking up at Ben when he was filled with passion over the Lakers in the play-offs?

I'm sorry, Grandma Popkin. You're right. If you have to stand up, I'm not speaking loud enough. I'll shout if I have to. *Who took my damned drink? Alice?*

Thanks, waiter, for the new one. At least you are with me.

OK.

Celeste, before you moved out to be with Ben, you always said that you were above the limits of relationships. You were on your own for good. But I said, "His eyes are nice, though, aren't they?" And you said you'd never noticed. You said that you didn't need a guy now.

Surprise, Ben.

Maybe it's my imagination, but, Celeste, it seems so clear that my dreams and your achievement seem so intertwined. I feel like an electron darting around a nucleus, solid and strong, sparking a color here, a passion there. And then you, Celeste, get the experience, and I get to watch.

Here I am watching again. It's OK, but what is it? Am I missing the boat, or are you happy only when you take something that somebody else wants, too?

No biggie. *Butt out, Alice. Sit it down, It's my mic babe!*

I haven't forgotten the poem. Hold up your glasses everyone like it's a toast! Here goes:

"Celeste is like a sister mine.

Our bond has been tempered by time,

And forever we vowed that we would not rely

On males, who might use us, fool us,

And maybe, even here and there, lie.

So how did we end up chasing the same man?

Was it an accident, or was it your plan?

Was it just as you always rehearsed?

A race in which you finished first?

But why should I be surprised?

You have been competing with me all of our lives."

The last line doesn't exactly rhyme, does it?

No biggie.

Anyway, maybe tomorrow when you and Ben stand under the wedding canopy in front of the rabbi, say those words, and exchange your rings, you might think about my little poem. I wrote it just for you, Celeste.

Ok.

Remember, I'm just kidding. It's all in jest. And fun. Right, Mrs. Popkin…Alice? Isn't that what you wanted me to do? Little stories?

I love you, Celeste.

Really.

Key Thief

I have been drafted by a Fischler family committee composed solely of me, an only child, to organize my dad Mort's home for his return from the hospital. Sweat is streaming down my cheeks from the exertion. Stale dog biscuits, bread crusts, and fingernail cuttings molder underneath sofa skirts. Dust balls everywhere. Should I have expected less from the lair of an ancient male?

My mom Sue, separated from Dad, is unwilling to help out in any way. When I take a break and plop down on the couch cushions, a cloud of incense and dog hairs well up in the air. They prompt a sneeze that I am fully aware is also tinged with resentment that I am working alone.

Ironically the heart of the job is relocating furniture Mom left behind. The one piece I can't budge is her prize armoire, a wardrobe as tall as an obelisk and as heavy as granite. It sticks halfway into the kitchen hallway leading to Dad's dining nook, an impediment to Dad's post-op ambulation.

Seen through the wardrobe's glass door is a teetering ceramic and silk Geisha doll, my mother's pride and joy. Crafted circa 1700, a mincing simpering caricature of femininity she stands two feet tall and appears to be reading the thick books on antiques stacked about her in the refracted light passing through the armoire's glass door.

I am afraid to shove the armoire aside and clear the hallway. The contents could tip over and the doll's porcelain head shatter.

And I can't find the armoire's key to open and empty it out first.

About a decade ago Mom declared herself fed up with Dad, then in his 80's, and moved for good to what had been their weekend cabin on Puget Sound. My parents never divorced.

My dad, ninety years old, hospitalized, recovering from his heart attack, is of course, no help with the cleanup or house preparation. The hospital therapists say that from now on he will only get around with an aluminum walker or - worse - in a wheelchair.

When I visited him last in the hospital, Dad's face was as pale as his pillowcase, a tag reading "Fischler, Mort," hung limply around his shrinking wrist. Dad stared at his wheelchair as he would stare at an enemy.

"I guess the sunken living room will be off limits now."

"What about setting up the dining nook?" I asked. "I could put your television and your book table there. And your favorite chair, the recliner."

"Maybe," he said. "They tell you when I get out of this place?"

"Dad," I said, "I'll have to move Mom's armoire."

"You know, I put that damned closet together once," Dad said. "It's like a giant puzzle piece really. The top unbolts and lifts off. If you are going to move it, be careful, because the door is hooked to the top. The glass in the door used to be a mirror. When I lifted the top for the first time, the door just fell, and the mirror shattered. I replaced it with the clear glass."

"Broken mirrors. That's why you had a heart attack," I joked.

Dad's brow furrowed, his finger on his lips;

"Not really. That was more than seven years ago. What a mess. There was glass everywhere." Are you sure you have to change everything, have to move that armoire?" His face was anxious for the answer.

"I don't think there is a choice," I said.

"Well, take the doll out first. It's important to your mother."

"The door is locked. I'll need the key to open it."

Dad twisted around on his hospital bed and tried to get his back comfortable.

"Your mother has the key; she took it with her when she moved out. She was worried that I might sell the doll in there—the antique Japanese doll. We bought it for thousands. In Georgia, of all places. She didn't want anyone to get hands on the doll."

Dad struggled to draw himself up on the pillows. "Have you talked to your mother about me?"

My mom Sue seemed to believe that animals were more loyal to her than people in general and me, in particular. She installed bird and squirrel food feeders on the decks of their home and cabin to nourish her beloved wildlife. Most of the feeding trays were made of cedar; the exceptions were the iridescent, red plastic hummingbird feeders. She had hung them within indoor eyesight from the roof joists of Dad house and from a tree branch near the cabin.

Mom would fill them to the top with sugar water that substituted for flower nectar. Three feeding tips like bent eyedroppers protruded out of the bottom of each feeder. Two or three hummingbirds, a tiny flotilla abuzz in the air, could feed on one feeder at the same time.

The artificial nectar seemed to form a liquid pearl magically clinging to each tip, bulging with surface tension, and shaking so slightly until a hummingbird would poke its beak into the pearl and drink.

I would roll my eyes in boredom as a kid when Mom repeatedly lectured me on the qualities of her fluttering avian favorites. With imperious authority she would read out loud over my objections from Johnsgard's The Hummingbirds of North America which she kept on a cabin table.

"The red color excites them, makes them curious, and they satisfy their curiosity by sticking their bills in the feeder tube. They return to the same feeding places year in and year out."

"I can recognize which ones are which," she would declare, "the females, the males. Fascinating. I can watch them by the hour.""

Mom once cocked one eyebrow at me, a signal that she intend to tell me something I should ignore only to my detriment, as if what she was about impart about the birds also should apply to me;

"They are known for their loyalty," she said. "Something for you to remember."

Two decades ago, as a part of making her life with Dad palatable, mom took up rummaging for old stuff that she called antiques. In those days she disguised herself in outsized sunglasses, leather miniskirts and had decked out Dad, ten years her senior, in bell-bottomed leisure suits and beads, also insisting that he grow bushy, white sideburns.

Looking like two escaped manikins from a costume store, they prowled the auction barns up and down the coastal towns of Washington and Oregon looking for bargains. Mom bought enthusiastically and eclectically recording in a notebook the uniqueness of each purchased item, citing its description in antique newsletters, magazines, or books.

Then overcome, it seemed, by a Midas-like fear that someone would take away her aggregations of silver, crystal, and china, Mom locked her self-proclaimed treasures behind closet doors, under trunk lids, and inside the giant armoire. If a storage container had no latch, she wrapped it tightly in chains bolted with Banham and Schlage padlocks.

When she abruptly and permanently moved into the family cabin, Mom left the stored antiques under chain and lock in Dad's home.

But she took the keys with her.

I rarely speak to my mother now; she lives in seclusion, accompanied by her two dogs. Although they spoke to each other weekly, Mom chose not to visit Dad in the hospital despite my urging that she do so if only to lessen my time there.

I believe that this was in part revenge; Mom regarded her separation from Dad as an opportunity for me to take her side, which I did not do.

"This is not the first time that you could have supported me and not him."

She was right; I believed that her leaving Dad as he aged was unforgivable.

Since my parents' separation, my cousins on Mom's side have informed me that she has suddenly begun remembering them with a profusion of letters and cards commemorating their family events, although she excludes recognition of mine.

Ironically, Dad's ill health has been the pretext for the little talking that Mom and I do, the catalyst, so to speak, for some level of intimacy, albeit a wary one on my part

When Dad returned home, I telephoned Mom from my car to get the armoire key while driving on the interstate in a soft summer rain. There is a pause in the ring, still time for me to hang up. Then there is her hello voice, guarded, invaded.

I attempt to give her current details about Dad's recovery but she interrupts to lecture me

"Let him go, Louis. He is ninety; he has lived a long life. Don't hold on."

Mom intones like a therapist while my windshield wipers click and scrape and the freeway slows, the drivers distracted by summer drizzles.

I continue to provide information.

"He can still live at home. With help, of course, which he can afford."

My freeway exit is ahead. The traffic flows out of the speeding freeway arterial like lemmings and then stops in a restless queue at a neighborhood intersection.

"Dad has to use a walker now," I say. "There is no choice. I've rearranged the dining nook so that he can watch TV and eat there. Now he can come straight across from the kitchen or down the hall from his bathroom and bedroom. The hardwood floors are perfect for the walker. He can glide between the bedroom and the kitchen. All flat flooring. No stairs."

A poncho and helmet-clad biker passes in front of me.

"There's one problem," I say. "The big wardrobe closet. The armoire in the hallway, it blocks the dining nook hallway."

"The high one?" Mom asks.

"The tall, heavy one with the Japanese doll in it."

"The glass face used to be a mirror," she recalls. "Your dad took it apart. Did you know that it comes apart?"

"Yes," I say. "I know."

"It unbolts. That's how they brought it from Vienna. It is Austrian walnut, and the top is screwed on. Perhaps Freud owned it. Wouldn't that be something? Freud's armoire, his clothes once hanging in there. And your dad wanted to put it together himself, alone."

"Yes," I say again. "It is locked now, and I can't slide it at all, can't push it without breaking things inside, I'm afraid. Dad says you have the key."

"Your dad couldn't handle the sides alone. I told him so, but he wouldn't listen. The door, that rounded door with the curved brown walnut edge? It held a beveled-glass European mirror, European craftsmanship. The Europeans made glass with great craft and care. There is no ripple in a reflection from European mirrors. No wobble. I was in the kitchen that day when the crash came."

"Crash?"

I can hear the barking of Missy, one of Mom's dogs; probably the squirrels are feeding on the cabin deck.

"Yes, a crash," she says. "The dogs jumped straight up in the air when the crash came. He lost control of the door, your dad. It just exploded, that mirrored door—an original European mirror from the nineteenth century—just splintered all over. I held Missy, because she would have rushed to the pieces and cut her paws.

"I told him not to take it apart alone, but Mort doesn't listen to anyone. He never has. You have to accept this, Louis. He never could listen to anyone. That is just the way he is. He is a strange man. I had the mirror replaced with clear glass. It's not valuable anymore, because the mirror was original and now it's broken, so that's that. The Japanese doll is valuable, though, very valuable."

"Mother, I need the key. I need to move the armoire. It sticks out into the hallway. Do you have the key? I can't find one at the house."

"Oh, I have the key," she says. "I have them all here, right here in the cabin. All on a single, brass key ring, an old jailer's ring I bought in Oregon—Medford, Oregon—at a swap meet. The ring is an original."

A car in the opposite lane has stopped for a woman crossing the street. I stop, too, as she lumbers across. Cars stopping for a pedestrian: common courtesy.

"Can you send me the key to the armoire?" I ask.

"No, I won't send the key."

I drive slowly here, trying to keep my thumping neck veins under control like the car creeping at a slow speed.

"Can you tell me why?"

"If I send the key in the mail, it might be lost, more likely stolen. I don't trust the mail."

"You could get a copy made. Keep the original." The clouds are clearing a bit, I think.

"I am keeping the original, believe me. But no copies. Copying could damage my key. You can figure out what to do without a key. You're clever at getting your way."

I remember that once in her many moments of disappointment with me, Mom snapped, "In this world, you're on your own; don't forget it. You get what you want on your own. You are clever. Figure it out."

My face grows warm. I feel an urge to bark back:

OK if you won't give me the key I will tear off the armoire's back, or better yet, insert a hack saw, rip up all that Freudian European woodwork, and whack out a section big enough to pull out your precious doll which I will send to you in pieces. If that is a bad idea, then help me by sending me the key.'

This tirade would be useless. It would do no more good than the rant of an infant trapped in a high chair. For sure she is wrong about one thing; I am not able to channel my rage at her unreasonable selfishness into some clever solution to move the goddamn armoire.

"Hold it," my Mom says. I can hear her rush across the room, her voice low, conspiratorial.

"There are two hummingbirds on the feeder tubes, sucking sugar water together, hovering there, the two of them, sipping, looking at me. I can't move, or they'll flit away."

The metro garbage-transfer station is ahead of me; I brace for the stench carried on the wet breeze. I can count on the odor the same way I can count on my mother consummating her revenge.

"Do you believe in reincarnation, Louis?" my mother says. "No, probably not. You are such a realist. But it is possible, isn't it, to come back as a bird? I can imagine it, though, being able to dash off above the trees to see everything for miles, to stop on a dime, to float in midair. When you get old, you can imagine being a hummingbird. You'll see, even if you can't imagine flying now."

"Maybe they only earn reincarnation as a loyal couple," I inaudibly mumble.

"What did you say, Louis?"

"I said I have to go. I'm here now at Dad's. We'll talk soon."

"OK," she says, and I hang up. Abrupt departure is fine with her; it does not bother her a bit.

My parents are dead now, strangely Mom first. I quickly sold Dad's house and all the antiques, cryptically noting that the amount paid for the armoire and the Japanese doll was a fraction of what my mother actually shelled out for them.

As little as I cared about the things that they left to me, I did wonder why it was that during my parents' lives I was unable to free myself from the conflict between them.

The night after the sale I have a waking dream: In the dining nook of his home Dad is standing near the armoire, his shoulders bent, his backbone curving with age, his right hand leaning on the wardrobe's solid walnut side, stopping and resting between steps, his face the color of mottled clay, his dark, circled eyes topped with white, brambled brows. He sees me, and holds his hand out, palm up, like a cop halting a line of traffic.

"Don't move the wardrobe—the armoire—please," he says, his eyes unblinking. "Let's leave it alone. Leave the armoire right here."

Despite his tiredness and his gray-colored skin, Dad's eyes shine with what I now see was his remaining hope. In my sleeping state I understand that hope. He wants to leave the armoire where his wife, has left it so that if she returns, even if only for a visit, he can blurt out, "You see darling, I have left everything just as you wanted it."

This was his greatest hope; that on his wife's return, his longing and his love will be clear to her because the armoire sits as she placed it, a silent monument to his vigilance and constancy.

Not moving the armoire has made Dad's moment possible; I feel my furrowed brow release. My breath slows.

In the dream I see a hummingbird outside the dining nook window flit to one of the red feeders in the search for a drop of sweet, artificial nectar. The beating of its wings vibrates the window.

Perhaps that dream bird is my mother, now freed of the limits of humanity, returning to her old haunts, peering through the window, her tiny wings whipping into a blur, inspecting to see that the armoire is where she left it, and with a shake of her feathered head and fueled by fulfilment, she can disappear into the trees forever. Maybe flight is possible.

The Time I Got an Oak Leaf Sticker in Printing

I was born left-handed. I reached for food left-handed. I buttoned my shirts left-handed and I zipped my zippers left-handed. And when was six I began to print left-handed.

The Latin word for "left" is "Sinister".

Mrs. Quam was my teacher in first grade, in elementary school, in rural Minnesota. My desk in Mrs. Quam's classroom was made of wood, and iron, and was bolted to the floor. Winnie Thompson who had two pig tails, sat behind me and kicked my seat all the time. The bench in front hinged to mine belonged to Carl Jurgenson who always wore corduroy pants that smelled a little like urine. Carl needed a bath; there were patches of grime on his neck that could not be covered by his blond hair.

Winnie and Carl were right handers.

The Latin word for "right" is "Dexter".

At first we all practiced printing together. The rough paper we used for practice sheets was light beige and had green horizontal lines about every inch or so. I would turn around and watch Winnie who made smooth rows of "O"s and "U"s that were even and plump. Winnie also made "I"s and "L"s that stood straight and tall like soldiers. Winnie's letters stayed inside the green lines on the practice sheets.

I saw what Carl was doing on his practice sheets at his desk because Carl sat side ways. When Carl printed on his practice sheets, his tongue snuck out of the corner of his mouth and his fingers turned white and red on the pencil as he pressed heavy black letters onto the practice sheet. But Carl never smeared the practice sheet during printing like I did because Carl's right hand was always ahead and not behind the point of his pencil. My left hand always trailed my letters, so my practice sheets were always smudged.

On Sundays I was taught how to print Hebrew with Claire Dubinsky who was younger than me and with Arthur Hirsch who was a year older. Our three families were the only Jews in the rural Minnesota town where I lived. I learned to print in Hebrew on Sundays just as I learned to print English in school on weekdays, copying the letters from large cards my father brought from Minneapolis.

Each Sunday, Claire, Arthur, and I sat together either at wooden card table with folding legs, or around one of the chrome and Formica tables in our families' kitchens. Sitting there together with Claire and Arthur, I printed Hebrew in block letters, just as I printed English in public school, clutching my lead pencils in my left hand pushing the pencil up and down on green lined paper shaping those strange letters.

On Sundays I printed from the right and not the left because Hebrew is scribed from the opposite of English. My left hand was an advantage in printing Hebrew. My hand stayed in front and not behind the Hebrew letters as I printed on the green lines. I didn't smear my Hebrew letters on my Sunday practice sheets. My Hebrew practice sheets were clean and not smudged. This was different than printing on weekdays, different than printing in school.

In public school my teacher Mrs. Quam often put her arm on my shoulder while I worked. Mrs. Quam smelled like the inside of my grandmother's dresser, lilac sweet when she put her arm over mine.

One fall day Mrs. Quam put her arm around my shoulders with that sweet old scent, and told me that I was going to learn to print like Winnie and Carl with my right hand so that there would be no more smudges. Mrs. Quam smiled when she told me. "Like everybody else" and "no smudges". Right handed. It sounded good to me.

Ms. Quam's desk was up by the black board and in front of the American flag. Next to the teachers desk there was a much smaller flat Formica table with one chair tucked underneath. Many times Mrs. Quam led Russell Bean, who could never keep quiet, up to the front table next to the teachers desk, because that way, Mrs. Quam could put her hand on Russell's shoulder while she stood by the black board, and most of the time that seemed to calm him down.

So I followed Mrs. Quam and that nice old lilac scent to the front table where she told me I would sit during printing, where Russell Bean sat when he was noisy, not at my desk between Carl and Winnie. Mrs. Quam gave me a special book whose pages had curves and letters for me to copy while I sat alone by her desk.

While Mrs. Quam led the rest of the class drawing letters from white charts leaning on the chalk board, I copied my curves and letters out of the special book Mrs. Quam gave to me. Not with the rest of the class.

Using my right hand, I tried to print the special curves and letters between the green lines on the practice sheets but it was no use. They would start there all right, but then my pencil would bobble up and down, and the curves and letters sank below the green lines like drowning boys sinking below the surface of a green lake. One curve or letter below the green line and I would lose another whole row. One bobble below the line, another drowning boy, and the whole row was shot. Only one mistake and I had ruined a whole line.

When I worked at the front table, Mrs. Quam would lean over me, just the way she would lean over Russell Bean when he sat at the front table.

"Now that's a good line," Mrs. Quam would say looking at my curves and letters: "that's improvement isn't it?" she would say, as if she couldn't see the drowning boys sinking below the green lines.

Friday was award day, the day Mrs. Quam stuck a gold star on the best practice sheets, the ones with even rows of straight lines and perfect round circles inside the green lines. She held up those practice sheets with a gold sticker on them for all of us to see. The gold star, there for the class to see, for Moms and Dads to see. Mrs. Quam stuck the gold stars on the practice sheets next to the name of the person who made those perfect rows. Then Mrs. Quam pinned the practice sheets with gold stars to the cork bulletin board next to the blackboard. Winnie always got gold stars. So did Carl.

Mrs. Quam also stuck brown oak leaf stickers on the so-so practice sheets. These were good too Mrs. Quam said; only a little improvement and they would be gold star practice sheets. Mrs. Quam gave back the practice sheets with the oak leaf stickers.

After handing back the oak leaf stickered practice sheets and after pinning the gold leaf stickered practice sheets to the bulletin board, Mrs. Quam still had my practice sheets. Mrs. Quam announced I that had been working to change my printing hand from my left hand to my right hand and that this was very, very, hard. Holding my practice sheet up with both hands and moving it so that everyone could see my mashed curves and crooked letters sinking below the green lines, Mrs. Quam said;

"Look at the improvement. There is real improvement here, Michael. We can all see the improvement, can't we?"

Winnie Thompson started to laugh and then put her hand in front of her mouth. Mrs. Quam went right on:

"Put your hand up if you think Michael should get an oak leaf sticker for improvement. I do." she said putting up her left hand.

I looked around; my seat at the front table was far away from the rows of desks. Everyone but me put up their hand and Mrs. Quam stuck an oak leaf sticker next to my drowning boys.

My week two practice sheets looked about the same as those from week one; so did my practice sheets in week three. In week ten my right-handed lines and curves still sunk below the green lines on the paper and Mrs. Quam gave up. My right hand simply was not dexterous. I didn't have to sit at the front table, Russell Bean's table, by the teacher's desk anymore; Mrs. Quam let me stay at my seat between Carl and Winnie and I was allowed again to use my left hand during printing practice.

The next year in second grade we were learning writing from Mrs. Bringleson, the second grade teacher. Like everyone else I wrote letters with slow slanted curves, learning to sweep the letters onto the pages. It was like sweeping with a broom, like waving away a fly, using the wrist to slant and bend the letters, no more straight up and down strokes.

Mrs. Bringleson let me write with my left hand, although my hand always passed over my pencil marks trailing behind and smudging the letters. But still I was writing at my seat with my class, all of us second graders writing at once, all of us copying off the same board charts at the same time, all of us writing and copying together seated in our desk rows, concentrating together, all of us sweeping the letters onto the practice sheets, examining our letters for their angles, design, and evenness, all together.

My class was writing together the day when Mrs. Bringleson began to ask each second grader what church their families belonged to, asking up and down each row of desks, polling and then writing the answer my classmates gave. Mrs. Bringleson started in the row of desks closest to the window asking the names of our churches. My row was by the black board, the last row Mrs. Bringleson would get to.

Carl said "Martin Luther" and kept writing.

Winnie said "Epiphany" and kept writing.

My left hand tightened on my pencil. I stopped sweeping, brushing, and examining my curves and letters onto my practice sheets. I didn't know why Mrs. Bringleson was asking but I had no church.

While I waited for Mrs. Bringleson to get down the row to me I considered that I might lie. I thought about claiming to be a Lutheran. Our next door neighbors were Lutherans and they seemed to be nice enough. I wasn't sure about the name of their church. I had been told that I had been born at Saint Olaf's Hospital and that name stuck in my mind. Perhaps I'd simply make up the name of my church when the time came and state it to be Saint Olaf's.

Ms. Bringleson never asked me what church I went to. She must have known there was no synagogue in our part of the Minnesota countryside. It didn't matter though, that she didn't ask me.

Not asking was the same as if the question 'What Church?' was printed on a piece of paper with an oak leaf sticker on it and pinned to my shirt, its curves and letters sinking below the green lines like drowning boys. It was as if my seat had a sign printed on it saying 'No Church'. I was as alone as when I sat at Russell Bean's table, feeling as separate in not being asked, feeling as if Ms. Bringleson had asked me and that I had answered. I was different again.

Left handed.

Sinister.

Lunch in the Courtyard

Bogged down in a swale of strange and arcane legal words during the law-school days, I suffer the same dream over and over at night. I am sitting at a long, planked table in one of Georgetown Law's dim nineteenth-century lecture halls, surrounded by a mass of suits, sport jackets, and ties. The bald head of Finckel, the torts professor, orders me to my feet to brief a case.

"Mr. Oberman," he says, "give me Baker v. US Can Company." The room is quiet and anxious.

My chair creaks as I rise and attempt to open my mouth, but I am unable to speak. My lips are stuck together. I try to pry them apart with my fingers and by blowing air out, but my upper lip breaks off in my hand like a chip of pottery. Noises like a bleating sheep come out of me in wet bubbles. With no upper lip, I have no consonants. There is laughter from the mass of students as blood spews from my gashed mouth onto my notes and my Black's Law Dictionary.

I awake and feel my face with damp hands. All the pieces have miraculously reassembled. And there's no blood. My smokes sit on top of my Black's Law Dictionary on the floor next to my bed. I light a cigarette and sit back against my pillow. I hear the first of the morning's jet airplanes bolt out of National Airport, heading out of the District of Columbia, the dwindling yowl of its engines leaving me behind.

I would rather book a ticket out. I would rather rocket out on any of those jets tearing out to anywhere, but I have no idea where I would go.

I grew up working in my father's dry-cleaning plant and studying the customers' fine clothes: suits, coats, and slacks of lustered woolen and cashmere; tawny plaids; thickened flannel and twill; sharply creased tweeds and worsteds' shirts cut from pure white and regal blue, pinpoint, oxford cloth; and ties of creamy silk in designs of swirling paisleys, patterned foulards, and regimental stripes.

The shop had a poster: "Clothes Make the Man." I believe this to be true. Clothes show a person's walk in life, forecast character. No one particular garment carries the whole message. It is the ensemble that warms me or warns me. I don't wait for behavior.

I decided years ago that I had a choice; I could clean the clothes, or I could wear the clothes. It was an easy choice. Now I'm at Georgetown Law.

It is springtime in the District of Columbia. Finals are coming, and the new body counts from Vietnam are reported in the *Washington Post*. We, the Americans, are winning the body-count war, and my draft board has requested my grades from school. If I fail finals, I will be wearing an olive-green uniform in Southeast Asia. It is much safer at Georgetown Law. Suits, sport jackets, and ties are safer than jungle khaki.

At noon after contracts class, I weave my way through the mobbed law-building hallway, past the six-foot-high painting of Thomas More in the foyer near the door. I can feel Thomas More's painted eyes follow me out of the granite and terra-cotta entrance as if he disapproves of my departure from class and study. But I want a smoke and some lunch before the afternoon's class on criminal law.

I walk around the derelicts sleeping on a hot-air grate in the sidewalk by the school's front door. The exhaust from the law building is discharged there and heats the bodies stretched over the metal bars. The sleepers give off the aroma of dirt and offal blended with urine, the stench of foreign gutters. Everybody calls the hot-air grate "The Georgetown Hilton." Bodies lie across it all day and all night.

I carry my *Black's Law Dictionary* next to my briefcase as I walk around the grate and the bodies. Black's is too bulky to fit inside the briefcase, but someone might steal it if I leave it in the law building.

Black's Law Dictionary is dense and stout and smells like authority. The inside page claims that Black's contains one hundred thousand words and phrases, accompanied by common-law interpretations as well as Latin roots and Anglo -Saxon pronunciations. The pages are thin as phyllo dough; they stick together, making it hard to read.

"Oberman, you can't go wrong," Sam Lerner, the bookstore owner, had said. "The law is words. And they're all in there, all of them."

I don't know the law, and I don't know the words. So I bought the *Black's Dictionary* from Sam. It is concrete heavy, the *Black's;* I carried the book out of Lerner's in both arms. I bring it to class every day, where it sits on the wooden, planked lecture-hall table. I confess, I never open it.

I eat lunch with two of my torts classmates, John and Larry. We sit on the grass lawn of the Court of Military Appeals across the street from the law building. The lawn is separated from E Street by a thick boxwood hedge and a row of cherry trees. The scent of cherry-tree blossoms seems to cover up the reek of car exhaust from E Street traffic. I see two marines in dress blues posted at the doors of the courthouse. Guarding the courthouse is better duty than Vietnam.

Larry and I carry sack lunches. John purchased a chicken-salad sandwich from the lunchroom Automat. I use my Black's Dictionary as a place mat.

Larry has an open New York Times in front of his face.

"General Westmoreland announced that the Viet Cong body count of the past week exceeds the number for the previous month," Larry reads. "Hooray for us. Where did I put my Pepsi?"

Larry wants to be an actor, but he needs to stay in law school to avoid the draft. Sometimes in the afternoon, Larry reads the Times' antiwar editorials and the military obituaries with a loud New York honk in the anteroom of the library. Larry graduated from Dartmouth. He is in blue today: blue shirt, a blue blazer—threadbare on the arms— and a striped tie, which is soiled at the knot from too much handling.

"As long we're out of 'Nam in two years," John says, "odds are my board won't take me." John's button-down shirt with his initials on the cuff is frayed at the neck. He sits on his sports coat; his club tie has brown gravy spilled on it. John went to Brown; he wears the blotched tie with pride.

Larry and John wear worn-out, *Bass Weejuns* loafers but no socks. My socks are black ones, nylon and cotton blend. I graduated from Colorado State University.

A jet airplane rips through the sunny sky. It is a 727 banking and rolling over the Potomac River away from National Airport. I could be out of here on one of those jets, out of DC, away from torts, Finckel, and finals. But I don't know what I would tell my draft board.

John takes my sack lunch, peers into the bag, and wrinkles his nose.

"Another stale-fish special from Oberman."

I pull the bag back. "Hands off, John. None for you."

John unwraps his flattened sandwich, removes the gum from his mouth, and bites off a wad of chicken salad and bread. He talks with his mouth full.

"I wouldn't touch your crap, Oberman," John says. "Tuna makes me upchuck."

Larry looks at John. "No napkins?" he says. "Talking while eating? I think we've given up on manners."

"Shove it up your ass, Larry." John's words pass through a spray of chicken salad.

Bantering with Larry and John—these two carelessly elegant, sockless ruffians with their frayed cuffs embroidered with initials, silk ties with food stains, and weary, worn-down, wine-colored loafers—makes my muscles unbind, makes my breathing slow down. Now I can take a bite of my sandwich.

A sleeper lies nearby on his side, his back to us underneath the courtyard's boxwood hedge. He is also sockless, and his cotton pants have a mahogany stain spreading across the seat like a Rorschach test. I can hear his snoring as we eat.

Larry waves his sandwich at the sleeper and says, "Another guy who couldn't stay awake in torts."

"Doesn't need to be awake," John says, talking and eating at the same time. "He's got last year's finals."

We laugh. Rumor has it that someone garnered copies of the final exams from last spring.

John takes out a Marlboro and holds it between his teeth as he lights up. He lays his silver *Brown lighter* on my *Black's Dictionary*. The lighter is engraved with crossed swords on a shield of polished metal.

The sleeper wakes up, maybe from our laughing or from the smell of tobacco. I watch him hoist himself to his feet and shuffle toward us.

"Hey, what about a smoke?" he says.

"Get lost, creep," John says.

"Not so fast, John," Larry says. His eyes gleam with opportunity. "This could be interesting." Sitting cross-legged on the grass, Larry waves at the sleeper. "You. Come here."

The sleeper is slow to hear that the voice addressing him has changed from John to Larry. He walks around to Larry and stands over him.

"What's up?" he asks.

"I'll make you a deal, friend," Larry says. "I'll give you a smoke if you'll tell me a little about yourself."

"Whaddya mean?"

"You know—where you're from, what you're doing here. Nothing terribly personal."

The man has skin like a brown grocery bag, and his teeth are yellow. He smells like a foreign gutter, like the Georgetown Hilton.

"Like, what's your name?" Larry smiles now, sticking out his hand. "My name's Larry." The man looks long at Larry and then takes his hand, slowly and deliberately.

"The name's Elbow," he says.

"Elbow? Elbow?" Larry asks. "What kind of a name is Elbow? I mean, how do you spell it?"

John starts to laugh. I have stopped eating; the smell of foreign gutters is too strong.

"You spell it just the way it sounds." Elbow's words crackle as if he were chewing *Rice Krispies* and talking at the same time.

"So," Larry says, "are you from around here?"

The man shakes his head slowly, as if he has pain when he moves.

"Nope, and it doesn't sound like you're from around here, either!" he says, jabbing a bony index finger at Larry.

"Ah," says Larry, falling backward as if struck by a spear, "My 'cultcha' has given me away." Larry is on a roll.

I light a cigarette with John's lighter and hope that the smoke will cover up the foreign gutters. I move Black's Dictionary out from under my lunch bag.

"Mr. Elbow," Larry says, "if I may I call you that, do you have a family?"

"I do," Elbow says, his hair sticking up on one side as if there is a cyclone blowing in the courtyard.

"Where are they?"

"Down in m' home."

"Where's that?"

"In Ashford. Ashford, North Carolina." Elbow points the wrong way; he points north, toward Maryland.

"Have kids?"

"Yup." He grins. "Three of them: two girls and a boy. Now what about that cigarette?"

"Yes, what about the cigarette, John?" Larry is being the ring impresario.

John tosses over the Marlboro pack. Larry takes one out and extends it to Elbow.

"How about a couple for my buddies?" Elbow says.

Larry feigns surprise and disappointment and says, "Mr. Elbow, we—you and I—had no arrangement for additional smokes. You're renegotiating our deal. What do we do about this? What about a tuna-fish sandwich?"

I snatch my sack away from Larry's hands.

"No way," Elbow says. "Not good for ya." He puts the Marlboro in his mouth. "Somebody gotta light?"

"Here." Larry throws over John's silver lighter.

"Gimme that back, asshole," John says to Larry.

"Too late, my boy," Larry says. "Need help in the operation, Elbow?"

Elbow pops open the lid, and the lighter ignites like a blowtorch.

"This is something," Elbow says, squinting through the smoke as the sun reflects off the silver lighter. The blend of Elbow's breath and smoke swirls around me like a dust devil on a newly plowed field.

"OK. Now let's have the lighter back, buddy," says John.

Elbow hands it over. "Thanks."

"Thanks for nothing," John says as he grabs the lighter from Elbow.

"Mr. Elbow," Larry says, "I have a new proposition for your consideration, and possibly I can offer some further benefits."

"Money," Elbow says. "You got some change for me?"

"I was thinking about the full pack of cigarettes, Mr. Elbow. No money."

Elbow now is hunkered down; the rubber is returning to his skin, and his balance is improving. He seems to enjoy the banter too.

"What for?" he says.

"Elbow," Larry says—dropping the "mister"—"Elbow, I don't understand. You have a wife, a family, children of your seed, a wonderful place you can call home. Why are you here in the District, sleeping in the grass and dew of the justice system, somewhat unclean and uncomfortable?"

Elbow rises halfway up. He stares at Larry's smile, as if he senses the possibility of a blow from his interrogator.

"Because," Elbow says with emphasis. He says it again. "Because."

"Because, why?" Larry asks.

"Because," Elbow repeats loudly and slowly, incredulous at the question and the accumulated impertinence of the questioner. Then he straightens up and speaks over the noise of cars going by on E Street.

"Because I'm a drunk," he says and stands there.

Larry and John are silent. I find myself unable to answer Larry's question that is now saturating the air around me: Why am I here?

Larry breaks the silence.

"This is bullshit. I'm done with this." He rises without acknowledging Elbow, who stands next to him.

"Larry, you've left your lunch crap," I say.

"You clean it up, Oberman," Larry says over his shoulder as he walks out of the courtyard.

Elbow says, "What about my smokes?"

There are grass patches on my pants from sitting on the lawn. Soiled, I think. Maybe stained forever.

I pick up *Black's Dictionary*. "Here, take this," I say, handing Elbow the Black's. "You can sell it to the bookstore owner over on the corner."

I point to Sam Lerner's bookstore across from the law school.

"Come on, Oberman," John says. "Don't kid the guy around."

"I'm not," I say. "This book is a waste, dead weight. I'm just lightening up."

"That book's a ticket to jail," Elbow says. "I walk in the store with that, and the book guy, he calls the cops."

"See, Oberman," says John, "this guy is better equipped to make it around here than you are."

He is right. Elbow knows that anyone with *Black's* in their hands looks like a phony. I would get off so easily by giving Black's to Elbow, but he won't take it.

I will have to buy my own plane ticket out of here. I will have to figure out where the planes leaving DC are going.

And deal with my draft board too. It is my draft board, after all.

A Winter Dance at Abruzzi's

Behind the bar at Abruzzi's Tavern in the one-street hamlet of Elgin, Minnesota, Nancy Lee Adams played at cleaning the counter with a rag dampened by spilled beer. Behind the bar, a Mitsubishi TV was mounted above the mirror. It was Thursday night, and as usual Nancy Lee had turned to the Nashville Channel's Dance Hall show. The dancers up there on the screen danced the Texas freeze in long lines while the DJ spun a Clint Black tune. Nancy Lee wiped away to the rhythm and bobbed her head when she heard the hitch in Clint's voice. And below the counter, her aging Nike cross-trainers did a minifreeze, Nancy joining the TV dancers from the knees on down.

It was one hour before Nancy Lee would close Abruzzi's, and the last customer, Harvey Nelskog, sat smoking a cigarette as he nursed a schooner of beer. The Nelskogs and Adamses were Elgin neighbors of long standing; when he was a little boy, Harvey's bedroom window had looked at the Adamses' porch.

The lit end of Harvey's cigarette sneaked off the ashtray's side. It slowly decomposed into a charcoal-colored slag pile on Abruzzi's mahogany bar. Originally an old-fashioned saloon top, sun-sprayed auburn, the jungle wood was now buried under a sea of plastic, leaving it bleary and glazed, although here and there scrapes from sliding glasses and ashtrays exposed the grain underneath, its texture warm, like the embers of a fire.

Past the soft cigarette ash spreading about on the bar top and outside the tavern's windows, a white prairie blizzard brewed. Since dusk, flurries of snowflakes—the shock troops of a fresh gale—swept off the lake and hurtled unimpeded across the Minnesota farmlands until they hit the tavern's walls. Each gust was reported with a slam of Abruzzi's loose screen door and a momentary dimming of the tavern's lights, as the power lines outside swayed and bent in the wind.

Nancy glided past the beer taps uninterrupted, as if there were no storm about to arrive. She could see her reflection in the mirror. Her curly, dark hair was in place, but the white at her temples was another story—wanting, as it did, to shoot off like ragweed in summer, independent and unsocial.

In midstep she peered at the bar rag's wet trail left on the counter and Harvey's ash puddle. Harvey was asleep, his eyelids wilted shut, anesthetized by beer and gravity. She began to form words of reproach and then stopped.

A waste of time, she thought, tossing down the bar rag and leaving the ash where it had dripped.

Gliding to the till, her feet keeping time to the music, Nancy Lee counted the night's meager take and reconciled it with the sales receipts. Abruzzi perpetually crabbed that Nancy Lee did not have a clue if the cash equaled sales. This night Abruzzi won, and she covered the cash shortage out of the little wad of ones and loose change stuffed in her bar's tip glass; on other nights when the register was fat with bills, she would move some dough into the tip glass.

It squares overall, I guess, she reckoned.

Up on the screen, a pair of white, soft-leather cowboy boots on one of the Texas girls caught Nancy Lee's eye. Just like a pair in the window down the street at Schwartz's Western Wear.

I could slip on those boots and walk into one of those clubs with giant TV screens everywhere, she thought. I would still be light as a feather, waving my hips on the turns, gliding on my tiptoes, the camera swinging overhead, picking me up and onto one'a those big screens. I could be one of those dancers up on the TV.

Dancing had always been in her blood. She remembered twirling late on a summer day when she was five years old, surrounded by all the neighbor kids. They all seemed to be boys of her age: Allen and Eddie Bach were there, and Harvey Nelskog, too. He was just a little squirt then. And Charles and Dennis, the Gunderson brothers—five, six, and seven years old. Bad breath on all of them; they didn't brush their teeth unless they were held by their ears and dragged over to the sink by a raging mom or dad.

Twirling felt good. Your head went all dizzy, and the ground got bumpy; and you dropped to your knees and rolled on your back until the ground became still again and the grass wet the back of your bare arms. Everybody on the lawn going in circles, the dogs running around barking too.

In mid-twirl she had heard Dennis Gunderson yell, "Hey, Nancy Lee! What's under that dress?" So she had twirled her dress up in the air—five years old, and so what? Didn't they have older sisters?

A tug and the sound of a rip like a fingernail on a blackboard. That stupid James Erskine had grabbed at her dress for a look.

Hey, Nancy Lee thought, *that James ripped my pleated cotton dress. What did he think would happen if he did that?*

Nancy Lee remembered her dad emerging from nowhere like a locomotive and smacking James Erskine out of the way, her dad yelling like a maniac, grabbing her under the armpits, and lifting her up in the air like a rag doll. It scared her to think of her dad's face—all sweaty, red, and dangerous—growing bigger than a windowpane, looking right into her eyes. She had screamed, too, knowing that she was next to be struck. Nancy Lee could smell his anger on his breath.

"Never let one'a those boys near, you hear?" Her dad's face had been red, his voice like a rumbling truck, and he had begun to swing his big right hand up from behind Nancy Lee's bottom like a steam shovel. Open palm. Over and over.

It was mayhem with the dogs running around and barking their heads off. Nancy Lee's nose bled; she became sick and vomited. She could hear her mom yelling too.

"Get away from her, Earl! Are you gone nuts? Get away from Nancy Lee, you wacko!"

But Nancy Lee recalled swearing to herself as her mom washed off the smear of blood and remnants of sour food that she would never stop the twirling. Because it felt so good.

The clock showed eleven forty. The Everly Brothers sang "Cathy's Clown" on the Nashville Channel while the dancers on the TV screen spun, stomped, skipped, and slid in their boots and ten-gallon hats.

"Get the Bronco fixed?" Nancy Lee asked Harvey.

"The radiator's in the shop," Harvey replied. "Somebody put a slug in it—a hunter, I guess. About one hundred and sixty bucks, maybe one hundred and seventy to weld it up. Can ya reach me some smokes?"

Nancy Lee took a Marlboro pack off the shelf and handed it to Harvey. The screen door banged three times in the wind. She thought of dancing in the empty light of Thursday.

"I always melt when I hear the Everly Brothers," she said, leaning her elbows on the bar, her chin on her hands. "'Dream' was their best; it was on the charts for two years."

Harvey grunted. "Abruzzi outa town?"

"Nope, he came down with the flu. You should'a heard him this afternoon. He was hacking like a circus seal begging for a mackerel. Figured he'd better stay in bed for a night or two."

"He owes me a drink," Harvey said. "Bet me that the ice would be off the lake by March fifteenth. Here it is the twentieth, and we're still solid as slate. I pulled the ice shed off the point last week, but we could'a been out there another month, the way it looks now." Harvey took a slug of his brew and wiped his mouth with the back of his hand.

Nancy Lee sighed. Abruzzi spent half the winter cooped up in one of those outhouses on skis—fishing line into the hole in the floor, propane stove humming—sitting there with his buddies, stoked on cheap bourbon, catching bass and pike, and then dropping the fish off for Nancy Lee to clean.

"Harvey, did you eat any of my pizza last week?" Nancy Lee asked. She had stacked the freezer so full of the winter's fish fillets that she was on the verge of having to throw out the frozen-pizza econo pack. Abruzzi had made her a deal; if she cooked and served the pizza as a giveaway on Thursday night, the worst night of the week, she would get a piece of the gate.

"Pizza was damned good," Harvey said and nodded.

The liquor sales showed it too. Before baking it, she had sprinkled the top of the pizza with a blast of Tabasco sauce. After a wedge of her pizza, you really needed some brew to knock the edge off. She supposed that the whole deal made her an extra fifty bucks. Clever.

So maybe I should have been an owner, Nancy Lee mused.

Winter flung the screen door against its sash again. "I wish we could lock that door," Nancy Lee said to no one and then realized that she had said those words once before in another time.

"I wish we could lock that door," Nancy Lee had said to Dennis Gunderson, standing by her front door on the house porch. It was two in the morning, her senior year at Elgin High. It was fall. There was a harvest moon, and Dennis smelled of Canoe aftershave. Nancy Lee could see one light inside the house near the kitchen.

Across at the Nelskogs, Harvey was staring at them through his bedroom window. Nancy Lee giggled, and she poked Dennis and pointed at Harvey's little head with the light behind it. Harvey scuttled away, and the light withdrew from the Adams' porch.

"Better get lost, creep," Dennis had said, "or I'll come over there and pound you."

"Shush," said Nancy Lee. "Someone will hear."

Dennis had left the radio on in his pickup. "There's something we can do in my wheels we can't do out here," he said. "Let's go for a ride."

Nancy Lee could hear the pickup radio and recognized the Five Satins singing "In the Still of the Night." It was a faraway sound in the dark, maybe hundreds of miles away, as far away as the Twin Cities where the radio signals started. Listening to the song as she stood there on the porch in the moonlight, Nancy Lee thought that she might want to dance with Dennis, might want to rub her cheek up against his while they danced.

"There's something we can do here and not there," she said. "Let's dance."

Nancy Lee came toward Dennis to do the two-step. She held her hands out ballroom-style.

"I won't bite you," she said.

Dennis was a soulless dancer, clumsy on his feet, but they danced together better that night than she thought they could—both conscious of their steps, feet closer than any other body part, feet alongside their partner's, tennis shoes brushing soap-and-water saddles, balls of the feet sliding back and then slipping sideways and then stepping forward again.

They held their weight in fragile balance, moving their bodies to the music and rhythm from the toes on up, their heels never touching the floor while the music was playing, while the Five Satins sang in the harmonic moonlight. Sometimes their thighs would touch, they would collide in embarrassment, and they would mutter, "Sorry," "Oops," or "Oh, not again!" All the time they held somewhat-damp hands, their arms around shoulders, a hand resting on hips, a hand in the small of the back.

Nancy Lee had this insatiable curiosity about Dennis's real contours. The bodies inside their garments seemed so remarkably different then. They danced closer until they collided together against the house, the button of the doorbell sticking into Nancy's behind and the chimes clamoring in the hallway, just as Dennis was reaching underneath her pleated dress.

The chimes cried out, and Nancy Lee said, "Shush," but it was too late. Her dad stepped to the door.

"What ya doin' with my daughter, you alley cat?" He was fatter—her dad—balder and redder than when Nancy Lee was five.

"Stay inside, Daddy," Nancy Lee said. "We aren't doing anything."

"I'll show you to hang around my house." Her dad flung the screen door open as Dennis ran to his truck.

"Lock the door!" Nancy Lee shouted, but she tore off the porch and ran after her dad. She had no plan as she jumped on his back before he reached the street—just to catch him by surprise. They blundered together and went down, landing in the cold gravel of the driveway. Her dad had smelled of day-old beer and body odor. The air and anger had gone out of him, but she didn't care. She shoved at him with the heel of her hand.

"Get outa here! Get outa here!" Nancy Lee wailed, her knees bloodied by the gravel. It was as if her dad had tried to stop her from dancing again, as if the porch had been her inner sanctum, as if they had not been out in the street under the Minnesota harvest moon where anybody could see them.

And in the spring she had married Dennis, the first of her three marriages to country boys who could not dance a lick.

★

Harvey shifted off his stool, his stomach hanging out over his belt. "Time to go," he said.

As Nancy Lee came around the bar, she took off her apron to the two-step. She held her hands out ballroom-style.

"Harvey, did you ever want to dance?" Nancy Lee asked. The music on the Nashville Channel was not right for close dancing, not right at all, but Nancy Lee didn't mind.

"Me? What on earth are you asking me that for?"

"I won't bite you," she said. They had been children together.

The music coming from the TV stopped. Harvey pushed his arms into his sheepskin coat and made for the door.

"Tell Abruzzi I ain't forgot about the bet," he said, wrapping the collar around his neck. He opened the front door, shoved aside the loose screen, and disappeared into the storm, leaving behind a deadly, floating cold that wound around Nancy Lee's ankles.

Nancy Lee rang up the register in the dull, yellow light remaining in the lounge. As an afterthought, she flushed the toilet to make sure that the water wouldn't freeze solid. She put on her coat, took a six-pack out of the fridge, and set it on the mahogany counter top.

Then, before opening the front door, Nancy Lee began to twirl, her pleated skirts opening up a little in the blinking red and orange light of the jukebox, showing off her dancing legs to the barstools. They were strong legs, not new but still muscled in the calves and thighs. They propelled her body around and around with balance and spun against disappointment, against monotony, against the loss of time.

Nancy was dancing into another place, a place that was all nerve pulse and bone waves, her muscles plastic with rhythm, and cameras admiring each dip, each skip, each glide, and each spin. Nancy Lee did the fly and coasted into a float move, and with a shake and then a shimmy in her shoulders, she reeled about and surged on like a milky dandelion seed blown by the winds of October, turning round and round.

With a twist and a whirl, Nancy Lee popped open the almost-freezing door handle, pivoted about as the door slammed shut behind her, and with the six-pack under her arm, she waded into the winds of a snowy Thursday night and left the dancing behind her.

She Said the Paint Job's Cool

In June 1960, my dad and I went tire kicking with Smitty over at the A-1 used car lot on Highway 99 trying to find me my first car.

The right car.

We went on Sunday, when the Seattle Rainiers were on the road and there were only church shows on TV. In the Sunday paper, A-1 had advertised a 1953 Mercury V-8, a Ford Motor Company car, a two-door hardtop convertible. I thought that a hardtop convertible had a wicked look.

My dad spotted a car he liked: a brown, 1952 Chevy, four-door sedan with a straight-six engine and posts between the side windows. The Chevy was a turkey car to me.

"You'll choose your own car, Mitchell," my dad said, "but General Motors cars beat the hell out of any Ford car." My dad always called me Mitchell, never Mitch. My dad always bought General Motors cars.

I wasn't blind; the Mercury needed work. The paint job was beaten up, the color like a banana that had been dropped in the dust.

"It looks like it's been peed on, Zeigler," Smitty said. "Gonna need paint."

Smitty was a guy in our neighborhood who worked at Boeing but made a buck customizing street rods. Smitty had let me hang out at the body shop in his garage since I was thirteen. Smitty always called me Zeigler, never Mitchell.

The Merc's tires were bald, and inside, the rubber floor mat was worn through near the gas pedal. Worse yet, the flesh-colored seat covers had a piece of red, plastic tape over a rip where the driver sat. Outside, on the left-side rear bumper, the Mercury had a dent.

"She was sideswiped a little," Aldo Olson, the salesman, said, "but the frame is OK." The dent puckered the left fender, and brown rust spread like a weed into the cracked paint.

For all that, I didn't care. I knew.

When you rolled down all the windows, the roof would float above the windshield and the air would whip through the sides and blow your hair about like the top was down.

It was the car I wanted to be seen in.

Right away I used up my savings account on new tires, ones with thin whitewalls, and Hollywood glass-pack mufflers that made the exhaust from my car's V-8 rumble with heavy rhythm. It was as if the engine was running in the bottom of a well. That rumble was a nice, evil sound—a nice, menacing sound. My car sounded low to the ground, a prowler.

After I got my tires and mufflers, I cruised by Carol Webber's house a lot. I cruised slowly, my engine rumbling, all my windows rolled down, and my radio rocking and rolling. I cruised with my left arm on the window ledge, my head nodding and jerking to the music, as I tried to feel like my car, hard and on the prowl. I looked straight ahead through my sunglasses, as if I was not looking for Carol Webber.

But I was.

I knew that Carol Webber cruised with guys who drove wicked cars. I knew that they drove back and forth around Carkeek Park in chopped Fords and lowered Studebakers. When I shut my eyes, I could see Carol Webber sitting next to me after I cherried up my Merc. I could see myself driving into Dick's Drive-In, with my mufflers rumbling and Carol Webber sitting next to me with her shining blond hair and swells under her sweater. Anybody buying a nineteen-cent hamburger at Dick's would see us together and hear the music coming out of my car.

Thinking about Carol Webber sitting next to me in my car plugged me up inside, and I had to stretch to get my blood flowing again to my arms and my fingers.

As long as I had known who he was, Russ Parker had been called Parker. Maybe three or four years older and taller than me, Parker seemed to have an extralong shadow whenever he climbed out of his 1949 Chevy, a faded-blue two-door humpbacked coupe. Parker's Chevy was lowered all around and was sprayed here and there with gray primer that covered the spots where someone had stripped off the chrome trim and filled the screw holes with putty.

To make a buck, Parker and his buddies caddied at Twin Firs Golf Course. Until I was sixteen, I caddied there too. Parker never talked to any younger kids while we waited to get caddie jobs. He was always combing his hair and smoking Camels, running his black comb through his brown-blond hair. Parker's hair always dropped back down over his eyes as soon as he finished stroking it off his forehead.

Parker cleaned his fingernails with a switchblade knife, chewing through the dirt under his nails with the point. He called his switchblade a "pigsticker," and he took it out when the older guys were around, guys like Dwayne Bean, who wore a leather biker's jacket and had long hair too.

Russ Parker and Dwayne Bean called themselves Rinks. When I walked to the golf course to caddie early in the morning and thought that Rinks, like Parker and Dwayne Bean, might drive by on the way, I would walk behind the trees next to the road. I would walk low and watch the ground.

Each morning the caddies drew from a card deck to see who would get the first jobs. The higher the card you drew, the higher you were on the list, and the sooner you got a job. The Rinks, wearing black leather biker's jackets, always pushed to the front of the line and picked cards first.

At one card draw, Parker drew low—only a four of clubs—and I drew high—the king. Parker grabbed my king.

"Hey," I said, "that's mine."

"You owe me a card, Mole." Parker called me one thing—Mole—although I don't know why.

Parker tossed the four into his shadow on the ground.

"Better take the four, Mole," he said. I picked up the four lying in Parker's shadow and didn't say anything. After that, I tried not to look at Parker's face when he was around.

After I was sixteen and had my Merc, I worked at my dad's hardware store across the street from Larry's Shell station. Steve Moffit, a guy I went to school with, worked at Larry's. Everybody called him Moffit.

Moffit pumped gas, cleaned windows, and checked oil. From my dad's store, I watched Moffit talking to Carol

Webber when she drove her dad's Pontiac up to Larry's Shell. Carol Webber was always driving around with her friend Annette Hurst. Annette had dark hair and worked at Spud's Fish and Chips.

Parker and Dwayne Bean also bought gas at Larry's for Parker's lowered '49 humpback Chevy. I watched Parker talk to Moffit at the gas pumps, even though Moffit was my age.

Moffit played football and cruised for girls with other guys, but he never asked me to cruise with him. Sometimes I tried to help Moffit when he worked on his dad's 1950 Dodge four-door.

"Zeigler," Moffit said once when we were setting the distributor points on the Dodge. "Did you know that some Rinks beat up Al Ryan? Three of them, at Zesto's, they knocked him out. Ryan. Can you believe it?" Al Ryan was a football player, like Moffit, a quarterback and tall, with a crew cut and strong hands.

"How could the Rinks have knocked Ryan out?"

"Hit him with a tire iron, I guess. Anyway, that's what I heard. I heard they had to take Ryan to the hospital."

"Which ones did it?" I asked. "Was it Parker? Or Dwayne Bean?"

"Didn't hear," Moffit said. "Could be. I don't know. But it was Rinks. Rinks are crazy. They'll do anything."

Moffit shrugged his shoulders, as if that was just the way it was in nature, just as if he was talking about a wasp or a snake or about anything dangerous. It was just the way it was, and Rinks were just the way they were—dangerous and crazy.

I worked on my Merc to get it ready to paint in Smitty's three-car garage, just around the corner from Larry's Shell. Smitty had blue-black air compressor hoses hung on the garage walls, coiled and ready to hook into his spray painter. Underneath the hoses on the wall were pinup-girl calendars—girls in short, tight skirts and sweaters, girls wearing two-piece swimsuits and bright smiles. I thought the pinup girls were smiling at me when I hung out at Smitty's, and it was always warmer in there, even in winter, because of the smiling girls, their long, great legs, and their swelling sweaters, like Carol Webber's.

I couldn't paint my car until I fixed the pucker in my car's side. Smitty helped me fill the crease with plastic filler putty and showed me how to file off the extra putty and sand out the grooves and furrows with wet-dry sandpaper glued to a block of wood.

"Sand the filler real soft, Ziegler," Smitty said, "like you're feeling a chick's boobs." Too much pressure while you were sanding would leave a wallow you could only see after the new paint was applied. Then it would be too late to refill the wallow without repainting the whole car.

Parker came over to Smitty's when I was sanding down the filler putty with wet-dry sandpaper. I saw Parker's shadow cross my car. I looked everywhere except at his eyes.

Parker talked to Smitty, not to me.

"Saw Holmgren's Ford, man. The man said you did the color coats. Cool beast, man. Maybe you and I could work a deal on painting my wheels."

"Maybe," Smitty said. "How much scratch you got?"

"Busted, man," Parker said, "but I could be coming into something."

Smitty held up his hands like "call me when you do." I kept sanding the plastic filler in my car's crease, trying to stay level, trying not to make a wallow.

Smitty wiped beads of sweat from his forehead.

"Parker," he said, "hear the one about the guy who wiped his ass left-handed and beat off right-handed?" I looked up long enough to see Parker sneer and light up a Camel.

Smitty finished the joke like he was on a stage, his right hand in a fist moving up and down, laughing hard. "Until he looked at his hand, he didn't know whether he was coming or going."

Smitty wheezed when he laughed, like the wheeze of his air compressors. I saw the pinup girls smiling right through the joke too. I didn't get the punch line, but I laughed because it made me nervous to hear about beating off since I was afraid Smitty would ask me how often I did it.

But he didn't.

While I was thinking about beating off, I saw Parker look at my car. Just for a second, I glanced at his eyes and the bags underneath. Parker's eyes looked dog mean, and I knew he didn't think any more of me than the worms in the dirt behind Smitty's garage.

I turned away fast, my eyes back on the filler putty where I was sanding, but Parker's shadow came across the coiled hoses and pinup girls and clouded the putty hump on my fender. I could smell cigarette smoke. Parker was close to me. I shut my eyes, but I kept sanding.

"Mole," Parker said, "you owe me a paint job." Parker was so close he was whispering. I kept sanding as if I didn't hear Parker, but I did hear him.

"What did you say, Parker?" I said.

"You heard me, Mole. You owe me a paint job." Parker's voice was smooth and cold, and I kept sanding with my eyes shut. When I opened my eyes and looked up, the shadow was gone, and so was Parker.

Smitty helped me pick paint for my car. I wanted candy-apple paint—two coats of paint, the top coat a skin of clear, wet, living color sprayed over a metal undercoating—but I had used up all but $250 buying the new tires and mufflers. That was not enough money to buy two paint batches. Not enough to spray my car twice.

Smitty came up with a plan.

"Choose a solid color, Zeigler," he said. "No undercoating. We could do it right and not use up all your hard-earned."

Smitty and I started with a light-green paint because it went OK with the flesh-colored seat covers. He took a little of the light-green paint and poured it into a clear plastic cup. Then Smitty stirred a drop of yellow paint into the cup, swirling the yellow into the green as if it were hot and needed cooling down.

"The yellow's gonna change the green," Smitty said. "Changes it from duck-shit green to lima-bean green."

Smitty kept stirring and swirling, adding another yellow drop and another.

"Believe it or not," I said, "I like lima beans."

"You would, Zeigler." Smitty set the cup down and walked toward the garage's wall shelf. He picked up an open can off the wall shelf and scooped out a spoonful of metallic gold-colored undercoat flakes.

"Watch this, Zeigler."

Smitty winked as he sprinkled gold flakes into the mix of the light-green base and the small drops of yellow paint. Smitty stared while he stirred, one eyebrow cocked up in the air as if he could see the paint better from an inch farther away from the cup. Then he tapped a little more metallic flake from the scoop into the mix. To me, each gold flake was like a lightbulb flashing on and off. With each flash, I thought I could see through the paint to the bottom of the cup.

Smitty stopped stirring and said, "Ya see, we could mix a little metallic flake into the paint. Shouldn't clog the nozzle. Whaddya think, Zeigler?"

I took my hands out of my back pockets and rubbed my face to be sure I heard right.

"I think it's great," I said. "Outstanding. God, I love it."

I imagined glowing metallic-green paint poured all over my car. I imagined Carol Webber wearing a two-piece swimsuit, looking at my car, coated metallic green, and not seeing the metal flakes, not seeing the lightbulbs, but feeling the heat of the car on her face even when it was parked and the motor off.

Carol Webber seeing how tough I looked behind the wheel of my lima-bean green machine.

Smitty snorted; his hands had green and yellow paint spots on them.

"It still looks like duck shit," he said, "but it's metallic duck shit from metallic ducks. OK, then. We'll paint it with metallic duck shit."

"It's a boss color—lima-bean green—to me," I said. Smitty handed me the green stir stick.

"Stare at it overnight anyway, Zeigler. If it gets ugly, we can bag it."

I took the stir stick home, but the color stayed boss.

The next Saturday after we had picked out the lima-bean green color, Smitty and I got my Merc ready to paint. We peeled off all the chrome trimming. We wrapped the Merc's windows, tires, and bumpers with masking tape and newspapers until my car looked bandaged up like an Egyptian mummy in the movies. Next we rolled the mummy into the paint booth in Smitty's garage. Smitty had made a paint booth in there by nailing plastic sheets to the ceiling and by taping the plastic sheets to the garage floor at the bottom.

Smitty had painted hundreds of hot rods in his garage paint booth. The plastic sheets were smeared with car enamel. Standing by the sheets was like standing next to a rainbow.

Smitty took down one of the blue-black coiled hoses hanging on top of the pinup-girl calendars and hooked the hose end into the paint spray gun and the air compressor. When he switched on the compressor, it pumped air in pulses, like my blood pulsed when I looked at Carol Webber.

Before he started painting, Smitty put on a suit like a spaceman, and while in his spacesuit, he sprayed a green mist over the mummy, waving the paint gun nozzle around and up and down like he was directing an orchestra and the paint nozzle was a wand.

Outside the paint booth's plastic sides, I watched the mummy soak up the metallic green sprinkled with gold flakes. I stood outside and watched in the strong light, waiting for the change, while gold metal spray swirled around Smitty in his spaceman suit and my car wrapped like a mummy. The paint smelled like butterscotch and tar.

When Smitty turned off the compressor, the hose slumped and coiled in circles inside the paint booth. My car wasn't the same anymore—not banana-pee yellow, not primer gray, not a mummy. In the strong light of Smitty's paint booth, the metallic-flake lima-bean green paint shimmered like the sun shining on the grass through a lawn sprinkler late on a summer day when it was so hot that the newspapers said, "Don't water."

My car had a smoking glow like a beach bonfire. It was boss.

The paint had to dry for three days before I could take my car out of Smitty's. Then I cruised Carol Webber's house; when I didn't see her Pontiac around, I drove over to Larry's Shell.

Moffit came around to the driver's side and looked in my window.

"Guess what," he said, "a chick was around asking if I had seen a Merc with a hot, green paint job." He was smiling but with respect.

It's Carol Webber, I thought. She was talking to Moffit about my machine.

"Was it Carol Webber?" I asked. "Did she say she really liked it?"

"Said it was cool." Moffit nodded. "Said the paint job's cool."

Moffit passed his tongue over his lips as he ran his hand along the top of the front left bumper. "Clean wheels, man," he said and then straightened up, put his hands in his pockets, and looked down Greenwood Avenue, like he was expecting somebody.

"Maybe we should cruise Carkeek Park after work, at eight," Moffit said. "I bet Webber and her buddies will be there. Cruise the park; see what's happening."

My heart was hopping around my chest. Moffit had never asked to cruise with me before. Now I would be looking for Carol Webber in my machine as I cruised with Moffit.

"After work," I said. "That's cool. See you after work."

At eight when the sky was getting dark, I went back to Larry's Shell with Carol Webber on my mind. Parker's lowered Chevy was alongside the restroom doors. Wearing his black leather biker's coat, Dwayne Bean stood over by the Coke machine. Parker stood by the Coke machine, too, with a Camel cigarette hanging from his lips and his eyes looking like a reptile's.

Moffit had changed into jeans and a T-shirt.

"They're loaded," Moffit said, looking at Parker and Dwayne Bean. "No way when I'm that old, I'll be hanging around a gas station, blotto. No way."

"No way," I said. "No way, José."

Moffit climbed in the passenger's side. I started my car; my Hollywood mufflers rumbled low and deep.

"Lay a patch, Zeigler," Moffit said. "Burn a little rubber."

"I don't know," I said. "Maybe I shouldn't in front of Parker."

"Who cares?" Moffit said. "Peel out, will ya?"

With my left foot, I let the clutch out fast, popped it, and rammed the gas pedal with my right foot. The engine wrenched my whitewall tires around so fast that they screeched like a tree full of crows as we squirted onto Greenwood Avenue.

I looked in my rearview mirror to see who had watched us, looked to see if Carol Webber's Pontiac was anywhere in sight, but all I saw was that Parker's faded-blue and primered Chevy had left Larry's Shell station, too, and was behind us, coming up behind us in our lane in a hurry, much lower than my car.

I slowed down so that I wouldn't get a ticket, and I moved over to the slow lane. I saw through my rearview mirror that Parker's Chevy moved over, too, as if there were a line hooking our two cars together, as if I had pulled Parker's humpback Chevy behind my '53 Mercury when I had peeled out of Larry's Shell station, laying a patch of rubber.

Maybe I did something wrong, I thought. *Maybe you're not supposed to peel out in front of Rinks.* Rinks were dangerous and crazy, and maybe laying a patch of rubber set them off. Maybe Ryan had laid a patch of rubber when the Rinks knocked him out and put him in the hospital, even though Moffit said Ryan was OK now.

The stoplight at Greenwood and 130th, by the Bible college, was red. I slowed down and watched Parker's faded-blue humpback Chevy getting closer to my car, Parker not slowing down. Moffit started to turn around and look back, just as I stopped, and Parker's Chevy rammed my car. He didn't ram us that hard, but it was enough to make my lima-bean green car grunt like it had the air knocked out of it, and it was enough to knock Moffit backward. My chin bounced back onto the steering wheel so that my tongue went numb.

I saw Parker's face when I looked in the rearview mirror, and he was laughing so hard that his dog-mean eyes were almost squeezed shut.

"Why'd you do that?" Moffit hollered back at Parker's Chevy, like he was tough, but he rolled up both windows on his side, front and back. Quickly, I rolled up my windows.

Parker's Chevy rammed us again, and this time my chest hit the steering wheel. I tried to hold myself back in the seat, but the ramming was too hard, and my chest got sore.

Moffit stuck his hand up in the air. He gave Parker's Chevy the finger, hard, like his finger was a pigsticker, and he was snapping his third finger up like a knife blade.

"Don't do that," I said, but Parker's Chevy just rammed us again as the light turned green. I decided I'd better get off Greenwood and head home. I forgot to signal my right turn, forgot to look straight ahead, forgot to turn on the radio. My hands were on the steering wheel, the windows rolled up tight now, my door locked. I didn't listen to my mufflers rumbling. I wanted to make my car run away from Parker faster. My tongue was numb, and my chest was sore.

Parker's Chevy turned, too, and stayed a little behind me. The darkening night took all the color out of Parker's Chevy. Now the hump was all that stood out as Parker's car skimmed along the road, a night-painted black car on a black street. Each time I turned a corner, I could see a humpback shadow on the streets behind headlights.

"This is bullshit," Moffit said. "Let's fight the fuckers right now." But Moffit had locked his door too.

I switched my headlights off, but my lima-bean green paint job was as bright as the streetlights overhead, as if each metal flake in my paint job flashed on and off in the light. Parker couldn't miss us no matter what I did, unless there was a place with no lights and I could get us way ahead of Parker's humpback Chevy. It felt like there was a compressor pumping in my sore chest.

I turned my Merc into Northwest Place, a dead end with no houses or streetlamps to throw light on my metallic green paint. I turned my headlights off and watched Parker's Chevy coming up; I hoped it would glide by, but it didn't. Parker's night-blackened Chevy slowed and then stopped. I heard its wheels creak as they turned on the gravel. The Chevy's headlights shone on my car and then swung across the street, left to right, lighting the right road edge and culvert, where the dirt was loose next to the blacktop.

The Chevy, sideways at an angle, blocked the way out of Northwest Place. Without sliding into the culvert, there was no room for my car to sneak by Parker's Chevy, no way to slip out of the dead-end street. I turned my lights on and looked hard, but there was no way to get past the Chevy on the road. There was no way out from the back.

Dwayne Bean got out of Parker's Chevy, the collar on his black leather biker's jacket snapped up high. He held a tire iron, its crooked neck sticking out of his fist. He tapped the pointed end, the end you stuck in the jack when you changed a tire. That end of the tire iron, he tapped into his palm over and over. Dwayne leaned against the Chevy's front fender—just leaned back, his legs kind of crossed, and just looked at my metallic green car, just looked at me and tapped the tire-iron end in his hand. I wouldn't shut off my car's engine.

The driver's door on Parker's Chevy opened, and Parker got out real slowly and stretched.

"Mole," Parker said.

"Parker, is that you?" I said.

"Mole. You owe me a car, Mole."

"What did he say?" I asked Moffit. My heart was pumping; each pulse made my chest sore all over again and kind of cut off my hearing.

"I think he said you owe him a car," Moffit replied. "They're both drunk. Let's get out of here."

"I don't know how," I said.

"Well, I'm not sitting here." Moffit swung his door open and skittered over the bank of the culvert. Moffit was a football player, and he was running off toward the woods. Full speed. On the other side of the culvert.

Parker walked up in front of my headlights laughing.

"One chickenshit hits the road; one chickenshit still inside," he said.

Parker didn't walk exactly. He went from side to side while he squeezed his right hand into his jeans pocket. I saw him take his pigsticker out of his pocket, his switchblade; I saw him snap the blade into the air. I could see the blade's shadow, because my car headlights were shining on Parker.

Dwayne Bean started walking around the other side of my car, all the time tapping his hand with the tire iron.

"Hope you got your helmet on, stud," he said. Then he swung the tire iron, swung it hard, and slapped my fender with the tire iron. The blunt point ripped the paint, going deep into the metal. I felt the thud of the tire iron in my sore chest.

There was no other way after that. I pressed hard on the gas pedal, and my car heaved forward, my hands on the steering wheel. I headed at the back end of Parker's humpback Chevy to get away somehow, to go home, to somehow shrink in size and slip around Parker's Chevy blocking the street.

Suddenly, I was going pretty fast.

I heard Parker say, "Jesus."

I heard glass crash, heard my right tire creak and then burst, and felt my car rise and then sag against Parker's Chevy. The right fender buckled, but my Merc wedged past Parker's Chevy in the dark, scraping it like a giant metal rasp.

Parker must have forgotten to set his brake because his Chevy lurched forward, pointing downhill toward the culvert on the right side of the road. The Chevy slipped over the culvert edge, its lowered bottom sliding down the gravel.

Then it was quiet. My Merc's right side slumped. The light from my unbroken taillights showed Parker's Chevy in the culvert stuck into a clump of weeds.

Parker and Dwayne Bean ran over to the Chevy and tried to shove it out of the ditch, but it didn't budge. They paid no attention to me. My car sat there, running, my right fender a jumble of bent metal.

Moffit came out of the dark. He opened the right door in a hurry and climbed in and said, "Let's get out of here. Holy shit."

I tried to drive my car toward Smitty's, but the right wheel was flat and the fender slapped the hub as my Merc flopped up and down like a horse on a merry-go-round. After a block or so, I gave up. I pulled over on the shoulder near the trees, stopped the car, and got out. I started to walk to Smitty's. I walked low to the ground, my chest sore. Moffit walked next to me.

"Maybe you shouldn't have peeled out," Moffit said after a while.

"You shouldn't have given Parker the finger," I said. "Now my car's wrecked, and Smitty's going to kill me." I had been better off before Moffit had said he would cruise with me. I wanted to wipe the whole night away.

A Pontiac came up behind. It was Carol Webber. It didn't matter. I wouldn't look up. I didn't want to be seen just then.

Inside the Pontiac, Carol Webber was driving. Her friend Annette Hurst, the one who had dark hair and worked at Spuds, was next to her and rolled down her window.

"Why are you guys walking?" she asked.

I didn't say anything.

"Car broke down," Moffit said.

I stared at the ground, my hands in my back pockets.

Inside the Pontiac Carole Webber laughed.

"Figures," she said.

"It's not funny," Annette said. She turned back toward me.

"Come on, Mitch," Annette said. "Climb in the back."

She looked at me with worry in her eyes. I liked that. I could see that it didn't matter to her what color my car was. And I liked being called Mitch—not Mitchell, not Mole, not Ziegler.

I have to say, I liked it a lot.

Pigs

Agent Bobler, am I glad to meet you! Or are you G-men called "Special Agent"? I do love that badge you just showed me. The word "humdinger" comes to mind.

Either way, I sure am pleased that you're around to help out after that swindler, Arnold Weisenbinder, took us to the cleaners. Maybe it'll help me get my money back, although I'm not sure I could ever testify in court. I can feel a sweat coming on just mentioning his name.

And by the way, my name's not Gary. It's Harland, Harland Hewsbach. I know, my name tag says, "Gary, Assistant Night Manager." See, the guy who had the job before me here at the East Spokane Holiday Inn was Mr. Gary. And guess what? Gary's my middle name too. Well, the old Gary, he's gone now, but I've kept his name tag until they can make me up a new one with my name, Harland, on it.

I can understand the delay in the name tags and whatnot. All hell turned loose last week, if you'll pardon my French, when Arnold Weisenbinder and the Coral Reef Gold Mine and you G-men showed up at the East Spokane Holiday Inn. I swear, I had to hold on to the rail like a tornado had come to Spokane and slammed smack-dab into the Holiday Inn.

You ask if I been working here for a while? Well, I've been in the hotel-management business forever, it seems. And have I been happy with the Holiday Inn organization here in East Spokane. They have been good to me! They treat their people a lot better than the Motel 6 folks I used to work for. Where I am now is a long way from the Hewsbach family farm in Asotin County, and thanks for that. If I ever see another pig or a dairy cow, I'll barf.

Sit down, why don't you? I'll get you some fresh java. Actually, my new promotion to assistant night manager has really been something. I get home at eight in the morning, about the time Willa and the kids are just starting to move. Actually, having my dinner when they're having breakfast is a pretty good deal. The quality of the TV at that time is better for the kids, you know—news instead of all that violence.

Let me tell you, we got something we can really share together as a family in the morning. Willa especially likes The Today Show and that Matt Lauer. He seems to really know the score. And who can say a bad word about Al Roker? He knows everybody in America, it seems, and has really lost the weight. Shows what you can do when you put your mind to it. I think the kids are learning a lot from them.

OK, I'll try to get back to Mr. Weisenbinder, but background is important here. See, my new job includes being in charge of creative marketing for the nighttime at the Holiday Inn. The daytime stuff is pretty predictable, a lot of sales meetings. I can't even keep all the companies straight. And on my shift, you know, at five thirty in the afternoon, we're really just cleaning up the coffee cups, throwing out the cigarette butts, and serving the holdovers drinks in the bar.

Well, I came up with this idea (actually I got it from QVC television, which runs nonstop, I guess), and I told my boss, Mr. Eidler. He's been with Holiday Inn forever, I think—a real solid company man, you know, a by-the-book type. Anyway, I pointed out that we can really make a hit by offering church groups night use of the conference rooms for peanuts and still come out ahead. I reasoned those church people who go to meetings don't drink coffee and don't smoke, so the rooms and linens will still be clean for the next morning's sales seminars.

So, what are we out? You see, it's been kind of quiet at night since we closed the Disco Lounge. We never could get the big-screen TV to work right in there, but the straw that really broke the camel's back was the Kenny Roger's sex scandal. Nobody wanted to sing his stuff anymore on karaoke night.

Sorry for getting off the track. My boss, Mr. Eidler, is a solid Baptist and thinks it's a great idea. He calls it "win-win." That's typical of how quick his mind is. Always coming up with snappy slogans. So we put up the signs on the grocery-store news boards and in the nickel-ad newspapers, and sure enough, the churches start to call. Not all at once, but after we got going, we had a bunch rolling in.

And that's when Arnold Weisenbinder showed up. It was the night that the Pentecostals had scheduled a debate on whether or not Jesus would approve of bingo, or something like that. The Pentecostals don't hold with anything fun, you know. Well, there were only twelve people in the room, and three of them were asleep when I looked in at nine thirty.

Anyway, up comes this guy in his eighties with a walking stick, kind of squinty and bent over, as you can imagine. He's got on this ten-gallon hat and cowboy boots and western bolo tie, but that's not what made him stand out. It's this white-and-gray-striped Western suit, the kind with the darts and arrows sewn onto the shoulders, slicker than snail snot.

And this coat is covered with pins from every church in creation. He's got crosses, fishes, stars, circles, and even some butterflies. I mean, it doesn't matter which church turns out to be on top. If having the pins gets you through those pearly gates, this guy is a shoo-in.

Oh, yes, and he's got this suitcase on wheels, the kind OJ used to run through the airport with right after he found out his plane was leaving in ten seconds. But this bag's got huge red, white, and blue destination stickers on it from all over the United States of America. And it turns out that it's full of more kinds of bibles than Carter's has little liver pills.

When he sees my name tag, he sort of shuffles over and introduces himself.

He says, "Mr. Gary, my name's Arnold Weisenbinder, and I saw your kind offer of a nighttime use of your conference room. I'd like to give some of your folks in Spokane the opportunity to make an investment in the future that is guaranteed in ways unknown in these parts. I'll be more than happy to do it for free for three nights, and then on the fourth night, I'll be glad to pay the rent myself."

You can see right away that this is no beginner. Here he is talking about *free* when the Holiday Inn is the one doing the charging for the conference rooms, and Arnold Weisenbinder was the one wanting to use them. I wasn't born yesterday, but I was polite about saying no.

"Thanks for the offer," says I, "and the name's Harland. I do understand the confusion with my name tag saying Gary and all. But all the same, we're pretty booked with the Congregationalists, Baptists, and the Mormons for the next few days."

"I like 'em all, Harland," Mr. Weisenbinder says. "I'll be glad to work right along with 'em."

I should have known then what we were up against, but I gave him the names of the people at the head of those church groups anyhow. I tell him that if it's all right with them, I don't mind a bit. He thanks me and opens his big bag and gives me a complimentary Bible. King James version, I recall.

"I figure you can always use an extra Bible around the home, regardless of your creed," says Mr. W. with a big grin.

So the next night when I come to work, there are notes from the Mormons, the Baptists, and the Congregationalists saying it's all right with them. That Arnold Weisenbinder worked quickly.

The next two days, there're signs out on the road in front of the Holiday Inn announcing in big letters:

The opening ceremonies for the Coral Reef Gold Mining Company coming soon at the East Spokane Holiday Inn. Free advice, entertainment, and opportunity await for the astute minded.

I must admit that I'm curious, so the first night I go in to see what's going on. It's the Mormons' night at the Holiday Inn. Arnold Weisenbinder has set up in a corner with a booth. There's this big map behind him stuck on the wall; it says "Okanagon County Gold Mines" across the top, and there's a whole bunch of names: Heckla, Star, Sunshine, and Holly mines, all the big companies with their names in little print. And right smack between them in great big letters with red arrows around it is the name "Coral Reef Gold Mine."

Arnold is talking away at full bore. He has a stack of Mormon Bibles sitting there topped with a sign that says "Free" on it. People are always drawn like flies to honey on that one. And right next to the Bibles, he has laid out an ocean-blue velvet cloth, and it's a beaut—the same stuff that those classy circus-trapeze artists use to make their snazzy costumes.

Well, Special Agent, on the blue velvet are chunks of gold and silver. Big nuggets. Each one has a sign next to it with dates, weights, and dollars. My eyes really pop when I see that the gold ones are worth thousands. So I stop to listen to Arnold, and here's what I pick up.

"I been a Mormon all my life," he starts. "The Coral Reef's the oldest gold mine in the Okanogan, and I'm the proud owner. I hate the big companies who hog all the profits. I've got gold ore lying around on the ground just waiting to be smelted. But I'm not about to spend the dough to ship tons of ore to the smelter. No, sir!" At this, Arnold swats the table. "Too expensive. So I hired the best chemical engineers in the world to leach the gold out of the ore right up there in the Okanagon and save all the hauling money for the small investors, the little folks who want some security."

Now Mr. Weisenbinder slows down and looks around at the folks there.

"It's called 'state-of-the-art space-age technology.' And it works. I guarantee it."

Then he holds up the biggest gold nugget and winks, and one man yells, "How do I get in on this?"

Arnold smiles and says, "Come back early on Thursday, friend, but take a free Bible tonight and pray that there's some Coral Reef Gold Mining Company stock left by the time you get here."

I'm telling you, Special Agent, I was ready right then to put two hundred big ones on the line, which shows you how I felt about it. Well, Arnold Weisenbinder sets up on Tuesday night with the next church group, the Congregationalists. This time the free books look like Congregationalist Bibles, and off he goes like the night before.

Wednesday, it's the same old story, except this night he's got the Baptists eating out of the palm of his wrinkled old hand, and Baptist Bibles are flying off the Formica like bats in a belfry. I could swear I heard him say he'd been a Baptist all his life, but it might have just been my hearing.

By Thursday night at ten, he's got the folks pouring in. I was a little worried because the smoking and coffee crowd had reappeared, and I had promised Mr. Eidler that there were enough linens for the community college conference the next morning. The college types were meeting on the word "synergism." That word seems to always bring in a curious bunch. They are really hot to find out what it means, I think.

Also, Arnold Weisenbinder got another break because, that week, Spokane was warmer than a roasting oven. Of course the Holiday Inn's got great air conditioning, so there was quite a swarm coming into the hotel.

Meanwhile, old Arnold's got a new sign up next to the map behind his booth. It says: "Tonight only: For each Coral Reef Gold Mine Company investor, free education stock for the kids."

Arnold is signing up new shareholders like crazy, and I get in line, too, so I can plunk down my hard-earned. I got my wad of tens with a rubber band wrapped around 'em so I don't lose the bills fighting through the crowd. I want those extra shares for my kids, like everybody else.

When I get to the front of the line, I see two stacks of certificates with "Coral Reef Gold Mining Company" on 'em. The certificates look just like gigantic dollar bills. One stack has pictures of eagles on it where normally on a dollar you'd see George Washington's face. The other stack looks the same, except it's got pictures on them of women in Greek robes. They're holding torches, and one of their bosoms is exposed. You couldn't choose that kind for the education shares. For the kids you had to take the eagles.

I'm at the front of the line holding my roll of ten-dollar bills up in the air, and Arnold grabs my dough. Then, bang, before I get my certificates, Arnold's grabbing another investor's cash and then another. They're around him thick as flies on a milking cow in August.

I'm yelling at him, "Hey, where's my stock? Where's the free shares?" I mean, I was hot that he had ignored me. But, anyway, he did, and I was there screaming just like the rest.

Then when the action around Arnold is like the bets going down at a carnival dice game, the front door pops open, and in rips the county sheriff with all you G-men in white shirts and blue suits, which was strange in itself, given the temperature. There're the TV cameras, too. The sheriff grabs everything—signs, stocks, bibles, the blue velvet, and whatnot—takes names and pictures, and then leaves the place in an uproar.

I was upset, I tell you. I grabbed one of the deputies and told him on the spot that he was keeping my children from their educational future, but he just looked at me like I was crazy.

The last thing I see is Arnold Weisenbinder's face as some young hotshot in a blue suit, who is barely old enough to be Arnold's grandson, has him by the arm. Arnold's got a big grin on his wrinkled face like he's having a high old time. And off they go, just like in The Untouchables. Whew!

Special Agent, you could'a knocked me over with a feather. Willa calls me at eleven o'clock; she says the whole thing on Arnold Weisenbinder is on TV. It turns out that Arnold's been selling this stock all over the place, and everybody's after him. There're folks from the EPA and DOE, the environmental people, because he's been spilling poisonous chemicals in the Okanogan's creeks. The SEC's after him for selling shares of stock that don't exist. The FBI is after him for somehow abusing the wires and the mail (although I can't imagine how you accomplish that!).

And of course the IRS is after him for you-know-what.

The whole thing got reported on NBC, CBS, and ABC. Willa said to me there were alphabet letters scattered all over the screen. She said that it looked like the only ones not after Arnold were the NFL and the NBA.

By eleven thirty I had to sit down from all the action. My money's gone, and you know how that makes you feel. Winded.

Anyway, up comes a hotel guest from Oklahoma by the name of Mr. Whitlow. You need for me to spell it? No? OK. Well, it seems he's in the animal-feed business, and does he ever know the famous Mr. Arnold Weisenbinder.

It turns out that during World War II, Arnold had a big contract to sell feed to the military, who were raising, of all things, pigs. Apparently Arnold got into big trouble because he sold the US Army raw garbage as pig food. The pigs, of course, didn't know the difference. Anyway, the G-men had tried to nail Arnold as a con man, but he went on the lam and has been at it ever since.

So, Special Agent, tell me, the Coral Reef Gold Mining Company stock was garbage, too, wasn't it? I probably didn't miss anything by not getting those stock certificates for the kids. When it's all said and done, I bet the best you can do with those stock certificates—with their eagles, torches, women's bosoms, and all—is to wallpaper your spare biffy with 'em.

So, Agent, how about some more coffee? Looks like you're about asleep.

I'll wrap it up quickly. After all was said and done, Mr. Eidler wasn't all that mad at me, even though the linens were pretty beat up and the synergism conference the next day had to make do with bare Formica conference tables. But, mostly, Mr. Eidler decided that the night-conference business can be tricky. From now on we are just going with the church types. As usual, the man's right.

Anyway, I learned a lot from old Arnold. The fact is that rich people keep the good stuff for themselves. After all, that's why they're rich, isn't it? I mean, what's in it for them if they give their moola away to the rest of us?

The other thing is pigs. It turns out that what you learn on the farm about animals is pretty much true for people. If you're a pig, you'll likely end up being fed garbage.

As for me, I'm following stocks with the kids on the Business Channel. We get *The Morning Report* from *Wall Street on TV* when I get home for the kid's breakfast. It puts Matt Lauer and Al Roker in the back seat. And I think this time we are really learning about some good investments. Anyway, I hope so. That's what TV can really do for the whole family, let me tell you.

About the Author

Mike Cohen has practiced law for over four decades. He studied fiction writing with Craig Lesley, Tom Spanbauer, Whitney Otto, and the late Robert Gordon, and has attended Portland State University's Haystack Summer Writing Workshops (1992-96) and the University of Washington Extension writing workshops (1995-98.) His short stories have been published in *Streetlight Magazine, Adelaide Literary Magazine, The American Writers Review,* and others. His novel *Rivertown Heroes* was published in 2017.

Mike holds a BA from the University of Washington and a JD from the Georgetown University Law Center. He lives with his family in the Pacific Northwest.

Publishing Credits

1. Streetlight Magazine, "The Cantor's Window,"

2. Adelaide Literary Magazine, "Motorbike Man,"

3. American Writers Review Anthology, "The Time I Got an Oak Leaf Sticker in Printing,"

4. FRiGG, "Fallout,"

5. Umbrella Factory, "Lunch in the Courtyard,"

6. The Penmen Review," I Wrote a Poem for my Best Friend's Wedding"

7. STORGY, "Pigs"

8. The Furious Gazelle, "She Said the Paint Job's Cool"

Made in the USA
San Bernardino, CA
02 August 2018